P9-DND-644

FANTASY LEAGUE

Philomel Books
Published by the Penguin Group
Penguin Group (USA) LLC
375 Hudson Street, New York, NY 10014

USA | Canada | UK | Ireland | Australia
New Zealand | India | South Africa | China
penguin.com | A Penguin Random House Company

Copyright © 2014 by Mike Lupica.
Penguin supports copyright. Copyright fuels creativity, encourages diverse voices, pro-
motes free speech, and creates a vibrant culture. Thank you for buying an authorized
edition of this book and for complying with copyright laws by not reproducing, scan-
ning, or distributing any part of it in any form without permission. You are supporting
writers and allowing Penguin to continue to publish books for every reader.

Library of Congress Cataloging-in-Publication Data
Lupica, Mike.
Fantasy league / Mike Lupica. pages cm Summary: In Los Angeles, twelve-year-old
Charlie's skill at fantasy football gains the attention of both the local media and
the owner of a professional football team.
[1. Football—Fiction.] I. Title. PZ7.L97914Fan 2014 [Fic]—dc23 2014007442

Printed in the United States of America.
ISBN 978-0-399-25607-3
1 3 5 7 9 10 8 6 4 2
Edited by Michael Green.
Design by Semadar Megged. Text set in 11-point Mercury Text G1.
The publisher does not have any control over and does not assume any responsibility
for third-party websites or their content.

MIKE LUPICA

FANTASY LEAGUE

PHILOMEL BOOKS
An Imprint of Penguin Group (USA)

ALSO BY #1 BESTSELLER MIKE LUPICA

Travel Team

Heat

Miracle on 49th Street

Summer Ball

The Big Field

Million-Dollar Throw

The Batboy

Hero

The Underdogs

True Legend

QB 1

This book is for Taylor McKelvy Lupica.

One

HERE WAS CHARLIE GAINES, king of the pro football fantasy leagues even at the age of twelve, not just watching the second preseason game for the Bengals and Giants as much as studying it.

His mom had come in a few minutes ago and said, "I can't tell, are you watching the game or searching for clues?"

"Both."

As soon as she'd come in, he'd paused the screen, freezing on the Giants' rookie quarterback out of Ohio State, Rex Tuttle, as he dropped back into shotgun formation.

"I'm not distracting you, am I?" she'd said. Charlie had turned, saw her smiling at him, both of them knowing what his answer was going to be.

"Yes," he'd said.

"Talk to you after the Super Bowl in February," she'd said, and left.

Charlie had the remote on one side of him on the bed, laptop on the other. He pointed the remote. The game came back to life, the announcers' voices came back into his room.

All the company he needed when there was a game on, Charlie happy being alone with football. Good at it. He really preferred watching the games alone unless he was watching with his friend Anna, the only person he knew who loved football as much as he did.

But then Anna's family owned a team.

It was different with Charlie Gaines; he felt as if the whole league belonged to him, the players and their stats and where they were in their careers and how much Charlie projected they had left in them. Sometimes his mom said that when he dropped his backpack on the table in the front hall, she expected decimal points to come spilling out.

"How many leagues are you in this season?" she'd said at dinner that night.

Meaning fantasy leagues.

"Just counting mine?" he'd said. "Or all the ones I help my friends with?"

She'd given him a long look. "You still have time for real life, right?"

Real life to his mom meant three things: friends and school. And his own football team in Pop Warner.

"Mom," he said, "I know you think sometimes that I've turned into some kind of football geek, that it's all I think about or talk about. But last year I had my best year ever at school. And you know I've got all the friends I could want *from* school."

"I'm allowed to worry about my guy," Karla Gaines said to her son. "It's what moms do. If we didn't have worrying, we'd have to do more yoga."

"I'm fine," he'd said. "And by the way? How can you worry about me and fantasy leagues when you're the one working in what you call the world of make-believe?"

They lived in Culver City, California, where Sony Studios was located. His mom worked there as an executive assistant for one of the top production guys, still believing she was going to be a movie producer herself someday, constantly on the lookout for what she called the "right script." He'd asked her once, one night last weekend when she was reading a script while Charlie watched one of the first preseason games, if she'd rather have the right script or the right man, having divorced Charlie's dad a long time ago.

"Script. If it's the right one, it doesn't leave."

At dinner tonight she'd said, "I just want your life to be great, pal."

"It is," Charlie Gaines had told her. Grinning. "How can it not be great? It's football season."

Most football fans thought the preseason was a waste of time. You hardly got to see the best players, and coaches were afraid of getting their stars hurt before they ever got anywhere near September.

Charlie didn't care, he loved it all.

It *was* football season again. From August all the way through the Super Bowl in February, it was when he was happiest, when his life *did* feel great.

He didn't have to watch tonight's game alone. He could have invited Anna over, but he was going to her house tomorrow night to watch her team—and his—the L.A. Bulldogs play the Bears in Chicago. And he could have invited one of his boys, Kevin Fallon, to come over—Kevin only lived two blocks away. The only problem with that was Kevin wanting to do his own play-by-play of the game; he hardly ever shut up.

It was better with Anna. She focused on games, especially Bulldogs games, the way he did. Maybe it was why she knew more about the sport than any guy Charlie knew, certainly any guy their age.

Any guy except for Charlie.

Charlie Gaines knew real games the way his friends knew video games. And wished that Anna's uncle, the general manager of the Bulldogs, knew the league that well. Or at least better than he did.

The Bulldogs were an expansion team still playing like one four years after they'd brought pro football back to Los Angeles. They were so bad, still not managing to have won more than four games in a season, that the sportswriters and the bloggers and the radio host and the fans on Twitter liked to say that pro football *still* hadn't come back to L.A.

But as pathetic as they were, Charlie still loved them, not because he had to the way Anna did, but for the only reason that mattered in sports, or had ever mattered: They were his first team. And were going to stay his team, even though they weren't getting any better and looked like they might never get better—there would be Sundays a month into the season when the stadium Anna's grandfather had built for his team would be half-full.

If that.

One of Charlie's football fantasies about his Bulldogs? That someday Bulldogs Stadium would be totally full, of noise and excitement, for a big game at the end of the season, instead of just playing out the string again.

The other day Charlie had read a review by one of the sports columnists in the *Los Angeles Times*, read it because he read everything about the Bulldogs no matter how bad it was. And it was bad:

> **It was so important to our city that we got it right when we finally did get pro football back. Only the people running the team, the Warrens, have done the opposite. Gotten it exactly wrong. Thanks for nothing.**

The columnist was talking about Joe Warren, Anna's grandfather, the owner of the team. And her uncle Matt, the team's general manager. They were about as popular in L.A. heading into another season as traffic.

The Bulldogs were named after an old independent team out of the city's football past, the L.A. Bulldogs of the 1930s. Charlie had read up on them and everything else that had ever happened in pro football in L.A. until the Rams left for St. Louis.

So he knew that the NFL had thought about bringing the

league to the city when the first Bulldogs were playing, but found out that teams from the East and the Midwest didn't want to take trains all the way across the country to play a game, even if they were only coming from Chicago, which Charlie knew used to have two teams and not just one. And cross-country flights were still sketchy in those days. So the city didn't get a team until the Rams in 1946, and then didn't have a team for nearly twenty years after the Rams left in 1994.

Now they had the brand-spanking-new L.A. Bulldogs. Except that wasn't what most people called them now.

People had taken to calling them the L.A. Dogs.

It was because they just kept losing. They either drafted the wrong players or traded for the wrong players or signed the wrong free agents. And when they managed to draft the right players in a given year, it seemed like they always got hurt.

That column in the *Times* said that one of the reasons fantasy football was so wildly popular in Los Angeles was because any kind of fantasy ball was better than the grim reality of the L.A. Dogs.

Charlie Gaines still loved both.

He'd read somewhere that fantasy football was at least seventy-five percent luck, people comparing it to playing blackjack, saying that you could have your system all you wanted, but the game still came down to what cards the dealer turned over. Maybe that was true. Charlie was fine with the element of luck—what happened on the field after you'd made your calls on which players you drafted and which ones you might slot in on a given Sunday, or Monday, or Thursday night.

He'd take his chances with the twenty-five percent that wasn't luck. Then it *did* feel like a video game to him, like he was playing *Madden* not just against a friend, but against a whole fantasy league.

And he was the one with the controller in his hands.

Controlling it like a champ.

Then it was all about brains and study and hard work. About searching for clues, even if you had to go back into the past looking for them. And maybe something else, too, what Charlie's buddy Kevin Fallon called Charlie's "gift."

When Kevin would say that, Charlie would tell him it sounded like something he'd unwrap on Christmas or on his birthday.

Kevin would come back at him: "You know what I mean. You're, like, a genius. It's why I started calling you Brain."

Charlie would come right back at *him*, ask how come somebody who studied hard and aced a test didn't have a gift. Wasn't called Brain.

"But you ace all the tests in football. It's why I don't know whether I should call you Brain, or just Freak."

"You know I'm not all that crazy about Brain. But let's go with that."

Charlie and Kevin went to Culver City Middle School—getting ready to start the seventh grade in a few weeks—and played football together for the Culver City Cardinals in Pop Warner. Kevin was the team's star running back, already talking about being in the backfield for USC or UCLA or even Stanford someday. Charlie? As much as he loved football, Charlie pretty much thought of himself as a scrub. Backup linebacker last season, probably a backup linebacker this season. Special teams player, which he told Kevin was misleading, since there was nothing special about his game.

He had enough size, that wasn't the problem. The problem was he just wasn't quite big enough, or fast enough, or strong enough. One time Kevin, being serious, asked Charlie what he thought his best position was and Charlie had said, "Blocked."

"I mean it," Kevin said. "What do you think your best thing in football is?"

"Probably holding a clipboard."

This was when they were playing sixth-grade football. Charlie didn't ever actually hold a clipboard but did spend a lot of time on the sideline standing next to their coaches. Occasionally he'd have the nerve to point out something he thought they'd missed. But mostly he was there to study them. See what they were seeing. And what *he* might be missing.

Trying to learn.

"Information is power," his mom always told him, explaining that was why she spent so much time reading what she called "the trades," newspapers like the *Hollywood Reporter* and *Variety* that covered the movie business.

"You're in a fantasy league, too!" he'd tell her.

When he was playing fantasy football, and winning at it, and being called Brain and a wizard and a genius by his friends—or a freak—he wasn't the boy without a dad. And he wasn't the boy who wasn't good enough to be a star playing football, or any other sport.

He felt like he was the one in the movies. A superhero.

The rest of the world didn't always make sense to Charlie Gaines. Football did. Who to pick and who not to pick and who to dump and who to keep. Who was on the rise and who was fading away. Which numbers meant something and which didn't and how they changed from season to season and what *that* meant.

He laughed sometimes at the idea that this was all a fantasy, because other than his love for his mom and his friends, nothing was more real in his life.

Maybe his biggest fantasy of all? Actually having a dad to watch football games with on Sunday afternoons in the fall, or Sunday nights, or Monday nights, or Thursdays. The way Kevin did. And Anna did. The way most of his friends did, but not all. Charlie knew he wasn't the only kid in Culver City with divorced parents.

Richard Gaines had left a few months before Charlie's fourth birthday. And had never come back. And had finally stopped calling. It was why Charlie's memories of him were sketchy at best. His mom would ask if he remembered the time they did this, or the time when he was three when they all went to Disneyland, and he'd shake his head. He did remember the time when his dad drove him down to San Diego to see a Chargers game, remembered where they sat and how cool he thought the Chargers' uniforms were and how big everything looked to him. But not much else. Sometimes he felt like he really shouldn't be missing something—a relationship with his dad—that he'd never had in the first place.

One time he heard his mom on the phone, talking to one of her friends, saying, "As far as I know, he's still out there trying to find his fortune. But I fully expect they'll find life on Mars before that happens."

Alone in his room now with football, his mom downstairs on her own computer, Charlie closed his eyes and shook his head, telling himself to focus on what he had in his life and not what he didn't.

The game in front of him.

Not as interested in a Giants' rookie on this night as he was a thirty-eight-year-old backup quarterback for the Bengals, lighting it up in the second quarter now that the Cincinnati starter was done for the night. It was no secret that everybody who followed pro football seemed to think that Tom Pinkett was washed-up, even though he'd been the number one pick in the draft when he'd come out of Arizona and was runner-up for the Heisman his senior year, that Tom Pinkett had no more value in real football than he did in fantasy.

Charlie wasn't so sure.

He wasn't thinking about taking him in the draft. But stuff happened during the season, guys got hurt, especially quarterbacks, despite all the rules they'd passed trying to keep them safe, to make the NFL even more of a passers' league. It's why you had to keep paying attention, even in the preseason—*especially* in the preseason—because there might be information you could use down the road.

You never knew who might turn out to be your difference maker.

He turned up the volume a little, wanting to hear what the announcers were saying about Tom Pinkett, one of them saying his arm looked stronger than it had in a few years. It made things less quiet in his room.

Charlie told himself the announcers were all the company he needed.

The Fantasy King, trying as always to keep it real.

Two

THEY WERE WAITING FOR THE GAME between the
Bulldogs and Bears in Chicago to start, Charlie and Anna Bretton
at her house, Charlie's mom having dropped him off, saying she'd
pick him up later after dinner with a friend over in Venice.

"Woman friend or man friend?" Charlie said in the car.

"Woman friend," she said. "If it was a date, I would have told
you it was a date."

"Dating is good," Charlie said.

His mom made a snorting sound. "You try it sometime."

He smiled at her and said, "I liked that last guy."

"Not as much as he liked himself."

"You know how you're always telling me you want me to have
a great life?" Charlie said. "I want the same for you."

"I don't need a man in it to get there," she said. "It just took me
a while to figure that out."

They had spent the day together, his mom taking him to a loca-
tion shoot of a new action movie starring Vin Diesel about some
former L.A. cops who end up saving the city from the bad cops

now running the police department. Karla Gaines would do that sometimes, to get Charlie into her world for a little while.

And, just maybe, get him interested in something other than football.

So they'd been in downtown Los Angeles for what was one of the last days of shooting, at Alvarado Street, near Dodger Stadium, watching this great chase scene between police cars and Diesel. Two police cars crashed into each other, one blowing up in front of Charlie's eyes. Charlie's mom tried to explain where they were in the story before realizing that Charlie had stopped listening.

He was staring at one of the actors who'd just been running down the street.

"Do you know who that is?" Charlie said.

"Let me guess . . . Is he the one who used to play football?"

"*He* is Jack Sutton, Mom," Charlie said. "He didn't just use to play football. He was known as Sack Sutton when he was the best linebacker on the entire planet, before his knee exploded like that fake cop car just did."

"How could I not have known these things?" she said.

"Seriously? How could you not tell me he was in this movie? Did you see him go flying around that corner? Holy moly, he looked like he did when he was still playing, when you thought Jack Sutton could outrun cars. That was before his knee. When he retired, he said he'd probably be limping for the rest of his life."

His mom smiled. "I'm sure the producers will be very excited to hear useful information like that."

"He even looks the same as he did when he was playing," Charlie said. "Same crazy long hair."

"He's kind of cute," Charlie's mom said.

"Ewwww, Mom."

"Just sayin'."

"Sack Sutton," Charlie said. "Unbelievable."

"What is unbelievable," Charlie's mom said, "is that now I can't even escape football at work. And you can't escape it even for an hour." She sighed. "Oh well, may as well make the best of it."

She walked him across Alvarado then, introduced him to Jack Sutton, who used to get into so much trouble off the field, had been suspended so many times, that he'd never played even one full sixteen-game season. That was before he wrecked his knee, getting hit low and hard after he'd made an interception.

Charlie's mom told Jack Sutton that her son was the star of his fantasy leagues. Jack shook Charlie's hand and said, "I'm doing a different kind of fantasy now. And get to be a rookie all over again."

"Fourteen and a half sacks your rookie year with the Jags," Charlie said.

"You remember the half? Not bad, kid. They didn't officially give it to me until the next year."

"The boy's pretty smart about football," Karla Gaines said.

"Wish I'd been smarter," Jack Sutton said.

"I'd like to know what you just ran in the forty," Charlie said.

"Too little, too late," Sutton replied. "Now, if you'll excuse me, it's time I got back to my new day job."

■■■

Later, Charlie was in the den at Anna's house, having told her he couldn't believe he got to meet Sack Sutton. Anna remembered that the Bulldogs had almost drafted him out of Miami, but passed because he was such a total wild man, her uncle Matt turning out to be right for once.

"He's actually been right pretty often," Charlie said.

"Not nearly often enough."

Their game was starting at six o'clock L.A. time. It was one of the best parts about being a football fan on the West Coast, night games starting this early. It was even better during the regular season, getting to watch the one o'clock games in the East at ten on Sunday morning. It almost made Charlie feel as if he were seeing the games before anybody else did, like he was getting a jump on the whole country.

The plan tonight was to watch the first half and then squeeze in burgers at halftime, Anna promising they wouldn't miss a down. Her mom and dad would be watching the game, too.

Anna and her parents went to all Bulldog home games, watching them from her grandfather's private suite. Sometimes they'd even catch a road game, Anna either flying on a private jet with her grandpa, or on the team's family plane.

It was no great secret at Culver City Middle who Anna was, or that she came from a rich family. Very rich. Even for L.A. The Warren family, Charlie knew from his mom, had made about ten fortunes in Los Angeles real estate, going all the way back to Anna's great-grandfather. But Anna and her family didn't live rich, which was why she didn't grow up in Beverly Hills, or Bel Air, or Malibu.

Anna's dad worked at Sony Studios, the same as Charlie's mom, but in the public relations department. Charlie's mom had always told him there were only two main groups of people in Los Angeles: Those who worked in the "industry," which meant the movie industry. And those who knew somebody who worked in the industry.

So Charlie and Anna both had parents working in the industry, but Charlie never thought of Anna that way; she came from the only business that interested him: the football business.

"You know why I like you so much?" Anna was saying to him as the two of them watched the pregame show.

"Because I make you look like you're the genius in your own fantasy leagues?"

"No, it's not that . . . and I don't need *you* to make *me* look like a genius," she said. "Though I have to say you do have a better brain for football than my uncle."

"I can hear you, you know?" Anna's mom said from the next room.

"It's true," Anna called back to her.

"Remember that you love your uncle and he loves you, too," her mom said.

Anna said to Charlie, "I'd love him a lot more if our team would win some games once in a while."

"Still hearing you!"

Anna smiled at her mom, even though Molly Bretton couldn't see her. "Having a private conversation here!"

Anna had long dark hair and brown eyes, and though she wasn't as tall as Charlie, she had long legs. There were about seven hundred girls at Culver Middle, but Charlie didn't think one of them was prettier than Anna Bretton.

Only she never acted as if she knew how pretty she was, the way she never made a big deal—any deal at all, really—about being a Warren. But she did love having a football team in the family. Even a bad one. And loved that team as fiercely as Charlie did. Maybe that was why they got along as well as they did. Anna had plenty of girlfriends at school, from her class, from her soccer team, from the tennis team. But she always seemed happier with Charlie and with guys who loved sports the way she did.

"What was I saying before"—she raised her voice now—"*my mother rudely interrupted us?*"

"You were about to explain why you practically worship the ground I walk on," Charlie said. "Or something along those lines."

"In your dreams."

"And you might have thrown in something about my good looks, probably, and amazing sense of humor."

"Aren't you leaving out modesty?"

"I'm much too modest to include that."

"Anyway," Anna said, "the reason I like you is because you never treat me differently or like I'm some kind of freak just because my gramps owns the team."

"That's because you don't act like one," Charlie said, grinning at her. "Freak or geek." In a quiet voice he added, "Nobody likes to be thought of as a freak."

"Wow," she said, grinning back. "Thanks for the compliment. Woo hoo! Anna Bretton . . . not a freak!"

"What I mean is that you don't act like you think you're some kind of celebrity even though other kids at school treat you like one."

"My parents want me to live a normal life," she said, putting air quotes around *normal*. "Or as normal as you can in L.A."

"Except when you watch from the suite in the stadium that your gramps built."

Bulldogs Stadium, downtown, next to the convention center.

"Oh, that silly thing?" she said.

"Just sayin' that I like you, too. Doesn't hurt that you love football the way I do."

"And know as much!"

"Almost as much."

This was a game they played all the time, like a song whose words they both knew by heart.

"*As* much," she said.

"If you know *as* much," Charlie said, "how come you need me to win your leagues?"

"You know I could do it on my own if I really wanted to."

"Really?" Charlie said.

"One of these years I just may have to prove to you I can," she said.

"How about this year?"

"Shut up," she said.

"Look at it this way," he said. "You're way better at real sports than I am."

Tennis was her best. She'd been competing in tournaments since she was seven. She was also the best soccer player on her team, and would threaten every year to go out for the boys' team, just to prove that she could make it.

"You're not as pathetic at football as you say you are," Anna said. "Or have convinced yourself you are."

They were about five minutes from kickoff.

"Not as pathetic as the Bulldogs," she added.

"Maybe they'll surprise us this season."

"How? Gramps told me he may have to buy up tickets himself so the opener isn't blacked out. Like, a *lot* of tickets."

It was a league rule. If you didn't sell out a home game, the game couldn't be shown on a local television station. Anna's grandfather had done it a few times last season, including for the home opener, but had finally given up. By December there were just too many empty seats. Those empty seats as much a symbol of what the Bulldogs had become as anything else.

Another way for people in the media, even the ones who seemed to want the team to do well, to say that pro football *still* hadn't come back to Los Angeles.

Anna said, "Gramps's whole life, all he wanted to do was own a football team in L.A. He had chances to buy other teams. But he wanted one here, because he grew up and lived his whole life here.

He finally gets one, even willing to build a stadium himself, and now he has to sit in that stadium and watch it empty out by December like it's some kind of fire hazard."

"Couple of really good drafts would turn everything around," Charlie said.

"Only if they were like *your* drafts."

"I draft guys off what they've done in the pros," Charlie said. "Your uncle drafts college guys and hopes they might do something. It's not an exact science."

"If it was science," she said, lowering her voice, "he'd flunk."

It wasn't as if Matt Warren was wrong about all the guys he'd drafted. But it seemed like when he took an offensive guy, the defensive guy he passed up would become a star. Or he'd pick up a defensive guy and watch the next season as the running back he could have taken rushed for a thousand yards somewhere else.

And he still hadn't found the right quarterback for a quarterback's league.

The Bulldogs had been 4–12 the past two seasons and were going to be lucky to be 4–12 again this season. Fans weren't stupid. They were smart enough to know that this season was probably going to look a lot like all the others for the L.A. Bulldogs, smart enough to know why there would probably be more empty seats than fans again by season's end.

Bulldogs Stadium was not really a fire hazard. Just a football hazard.

"It's killing Gramps," Anna said. "But it would kill him even more to do what he ought to do."

"Which is what?"

"You know what. Fire my uncle."

"Anna Warren Bretton!" her mom said, standing in the door-way with guacamole and chips.

Even Charlie knew it was never good when her mom used all three names.

"We don't talk about family that way and you know it, young lady."

Young lady. That was never good, either.

"I'm right, Mom, and you know it."

"I don't know anything of the kind. We all knew going into this, starting with your grandfather, that it was going to take time to build a winner."

Charlie was looking at Anna now, seeing a face he'd see from her on the soccer field, or in a close tennis match. He called it her don't-mess-with-me look.

"It would be nice if that happened while my grandfather was still alive," Anna said.

"Your grandfather isn't going anywhere."

Anna turned back to the screen as the Bears lined up to kick the ball off.

"He isn't going anywhere and neither is our team," Anna said to her mom.

Then she asked if she and Charlie could go upstairs and watch the game in her room.

"So I won't distract the two of you?" Molly Bretton said.

"Something like that."

"Thanks for not sugarcoating it," her mom said. "You can bring the chips and dip up, just don't make a mess. Your dad will have the grill fired up and the burgers ready to go at the half."

"Hope our team hasn't made me lose my appetite by then," Anna said.

It actually made her mom laugh.

"It's only our second preseason game," Anna's mom said. "You can't give up yet."

"Watch me." Anna took the plate from her mom, and led Charlie out of the room and up the stairs.

Toughest guy he knew was a girl.

Three

THEY WATCHED THE FIRST HALF of the game, watched Chase Sisk, their second-year quarterback, throw an interception on the Bulldogs' first series, then go three-and-out on the next two, by which time it was 14–0, Bears.

But the whole time, even as bad as the Bulldogs looked on both sides of the ball, Charlie and Anna did their favorite thing in the world: Spoke football to each other.

And argued about it.

It was part of the fun of the two of them being together, a football game on in front of them, even when they were agreeing to disagree about the team they both loved.

"He should have pulled it down and run with it," Anna said at one point after Chase nearly threw another interception, in there one more series than the announcers thought he would be.

"No way," Charlie said. "He made the right decision, just a lame throw. Gilmore was open."

"You're wrong," she said. "He had open field in front of him. Should have run for the first down."

"Wrong? I thought you said I was the real brain here."

"Yes, wrong. Better get used to it, Brain. Your boy Gilmore probably won't even make the team."

Michael Gilmore, rookie from Tennessee. Charlie's new favorite player, just off the Bulldogs' first preseason game.

Gilmore was a fourth-round draft choice. Charlie had seen him play against Auburn as a sophomore, saw him make this amazing one-handed catch in the back of the end zone to win a game for Tennessee, had followed him ever since. Charlie loved that the Bulldogs had drafted him, even though the Bulldogs were mocked around the league for the way they'd been stockpiling receivers like Michael Gilmore since they'd been in business.

They'd been doing this even though the Bulldogs had never had a quarterback accurate enough or good enough to get all those hotshot wideouts the ball.

"He'll end up in the Pro Bowl one of these days, wait and see," Charlie said.

"We should have taken a defensive lineman. Or a linebacker."

"Like who? All the impact defenders had been drafted by then. Why waste the pick."

"We can't stop the run," she said. "We've never been able to stop the run."

"Our problem," Charlie said, knowing he sounded like a know-it-all, and knowing that would make her dig in even more, "is that we've never been able to score in a scoring league. Michael Gilmore will give us a better chance to do that."

Anna crossed her arms, shook her head. "We need wide

bodies, not another wide receiver. Did I mention that we can't stop a sneeze, much less a good running back?"

"Just because we've been wrong drafting skill position players in the past, doesn't mean we should pass up a guy like this, especially when he fell into our laps in the fourth round."

"Oh," she said, "he's got a position all right. Just not enough skills."

Grinning back at him. Enjoying this as much as he was. Never giving an inch.

"Here you are, always breaking down football like it's a math problem," she said. "But then you fall in love with a rookie receiver like any other crazy fan."

"I am a crazy fan," he said. "Doesn't make me for-real crazy."

It was just one of their normal debates. What Charlie and Anna would be doing from now until the Super Bowl.

Neither of them giving an inch.

In that moment on the screen, Chase Sisk threw Gilmore a short pass and he turned it into a sixteen-yard gain.

"Yeah, you sure know your football, no question about *that*."

Anna made a face at him. "Sarcasm is a weapon for the weak."

"What's weak," he said, "is your opinion of this guy."

Before long it was 24–0, Bears, and Anna reached for the remote. She muted the sound on the game, saying that the announcers were starting to annoy her. Something that usually happened when the Bulldogs were this far behind.

"Another stellar team my uncle Matt has assembled," she said.

Charlie wasn't ready to give up just yet. There were only three minutes before the half, the Bulldogs moving the ball for the first time all night, JJ Guerrero in at quarterback, a free agent from UCLA they'd signed during the off-season. Didn't have a great arm, but could move in the pocket, wasn't afraid to mess up his completion percentage and quarterback rating by throwing the ball away when he had to.

One more thing that Charlie knew about football: completion percentages and quarterback ratings could lie right to your face; you needed to see how a guy got to both. Look for the numbers within the numbers.

He wondered if the people in charge of the Bulldogs did the same.

Charlie said, "Can I ask you something?"

"It is going to annoy me as much as these announcers?"

"How'd your uncle Matt get the job in the first place?"

Anna rolled her eyes.

"Uncle Matt played in college, at USC," she said. "And he'd always done well helping Gramps in the real estate business, and with the sports radio stations they ended up buying. And it was Uncle Matt who did a lot of the negotiations with the league and with the city. On top of all that, I think Gramps had always promised him that if they ever did get a team, they were going to run it together, the way Jerry Jones does with his kids in Dallas."

JJ Guerrero missed with a third-down pass into the end zone, Charlie seeing that it wasn't his fault. Ike Barber, a wideout Charlie thought was already in decline only three years after the Bulldogs had drafted him, had been slow making his cut to the outside.

Before Charlie could say anything, Anna said, "Real barbers run better pass routes than Ike does."

"Tight end was wide open," Charlie said, "watch on the replay."

Anna made a snorting noise.

"Mo is open a lot," Anna said, talking about Mo Bettencourt. "Doesn't matter if nobody throws him the stupid ball."

The Bulldogs at least managed to kick a field goal, making it 24–3 to end the half.

"Not the most encouraging start to the season," Charlie said.

"Speaking of seasons," Anna said, "when does practice officially start for you guys?"

"Monday. *Can't wait.*"

Saying it in a way that let her know he meant the opposite.

"C'mon," she said, "you know it will be fun."

"For who?"

"You like being with the guys."

"The other guys can play. I can't."

From downstairs, they heard Anna's mom calling them for dinner.

"If you keep thinking that way," Anna said, "you're never going to get better."

"It doesn't matter how I think," he said, "I'm never going to be good enough. I don't run well enough, I don't tackle all that well, and I've never been able to throw it or catch it well enough."

Anna smiled at him. That smile, he knew, made her even prettier. And even though Charlie Gaines would never admit it, when she smiled at him that way it made him as happy as football did.

Maybe more.

"Well, look at it this way," Anna said. "If you're really that bad . . . you might grow up to play for the Bulldogs someday!"

They ate dinner and managed to laugh about the state of the L.A. Dogs the whole time. When they were finished, Anna's mom asked if they were going to watch the second half.

Anna looked at her and said, "I can't believe you even asked us that."

Charlie said, "Seriously Mrs. Bretton? Sometimes I feel like I don't know you anymore."

They watched the second half, knowing that so many of the players they were watching weren't ever going to make the team. The Bears ended up winning, 38–10. Charlie's mom showed up about ten minutes after the game ended, perfect timing. Anna said she'd call Charlie tomorrow, maybe they could go to a movie before the Giants-Packers game on Sunday night—just assuming they were going to watch it together.

"Your house or mine?" he said.

She smiled at him again. "I totally don't care."

Neither did he.

"We'll figure it out tomorrow."

"Hey?" she said.

He turned at the door to her room.

"The way we're obsessed with football, you think other people think we're weird?" Anna said.

Charlie was the one smiling now. "Probably," he said. "You care?"

"Not even a little bit."

When he got into the car, his mom asked if he and Anna had had fun.

"We always have fun," he said.

"I think I might have picked up on that," she said.

On the way home, he thought about something one of the announcers had said in the fourth quarter, about how this was going to be another long season for the Los Angeles Bulldogs.

Charlie understood what the guy meant; he hadn't seen anything tonight that made him think the team was going to get better anytime soon.

Or ever.

Still: As far as he was concerned, the football season was never long enough to suit him. He was already thinking about Giants-Packers. There were a couple of rookie running backs on both teams he wanted to see. And one of the Packers' best receivers was coming off shoulder surgery, and was expected to be out there for the first time since he'd gotten hurt last December.

One game had just ended and he couldn't wait for the next one to start. Six more months of football in front of him, as far as he could see. Like football was a family reunion with endless relatives he couldn't wait to see.

The kid without a dad feeling like part of the biggest family around.

Four

FOR ALL THE JOKES he made about his own football ability, or lack of it, Charlie really did love being a part of the Culver City Cardinals.

He loved being part of a team, loved being with his friends, loved putting on pads and a helmet. Loved being a linebacker, analyzing the offense before the ball was snapped. It was football, after all, real football, Charlie getting the chance to be on the inside of it for a change, not just studying it in front of a television or his laptop screen.

He worked hard at it, too, tried even harder, did everything he could to get better. He *did* want to get better in the worst way, even though he didn't admit it, even with Anna. Wanted to believe all the things that he had ever heard about football—or any sport— that if you had the passion and the heart and the drive and you were willing to work, you could become the player that you wanted to be.

But Charlie knew that the part they left out of that inspiring pep talk was the part about talent. And if you evaluated pro foot-ball players the way he did, if you prided yourself on properly assessing their strengths and weaknesses and then deciding how much they could help you, you had to be realistic about talent.

Charlie was just as realistic about his own talent.

He didn't lie to himself about the players he drafted and he wasn't going to lie about himself. Oh, he could use his brain on Memorial Field. He knew not only where the offensive guys were supposed to be, he had the ability to recognize where they planned on going. He wasn't afraid when he was playing outside line-backer, wasn't scared to trust his instincts as he read a play unfold-ing in front of him. And he was actually a decent tackler when he had the chance.

But even when he was in pads, the way he was today, his friends still thought of him the same way, the nickname Kevin Fallon had given him: Brain.

It was a nice way of calling him a nerd when it came to football. The nerd playing outside linebacker and special teams for the Cul-ver City Cardinals. The guy without speed or strength.

Just being realistic.

They had gone through two days of tryouts the week before, the coaches deciding which guys were on offense and which ones on defense. Most of the first official day of practice had been basic stuff, blocking, tackling and agility drills, the quarterbacks and running backs and receivers breaking out to walk through a cou-ple of plays.

After that Jarrod Benedict, their starting quarterback, and Kemar Brady, his backup, did some throwing against the linebackers and defensive backs.

"Just a day to get you into a football frame of mind," Coach Dayley had said.

As if I ever need any help with that, Charlie thought.

With about twenty minutes left in practice, Coach Dayley announced that even though they'd finished everything he wanted them to do on the first day in pads, they might as well have a little fun and do some scrimmaging, eleven-on-eleven.

Coach Dayley would handle the offensive play-calling. Kevin Fallon's dad, an assistant coach with the Cardinals, would take care of the defense.

Coach Dayley put the ball on the defense's twenty-five-yard line and told the offense it had four plays to score, no first downs. Then he went into the offensive huddle with his playbooks. Charlie could see him pointing something out to Jarrod.

In the defensive huddle Mr. Fallon said, "For today we'll just go with our basic 4-3. Corners take the wideouts, safeties you read the play. Charlie, you cover the tight end if he lines up to your side. You're gonna hear this a lot from me this season, but I want you all to read and react once the ball is snapped."

"Oh, and one more thing," Coach Dayley called out, stepping away from his huddle. "If the offense scores, the defense has to run laps. If the defense can hold all these fancy boys I've got here on offense, then the fancy boys will be the ones doing the running."

Now it really felt like football season at Memorial Field. And for a handful of plays, Charlie got to feel pretty fancy himself, responsible for the tight end, rocking it with the first stringers.

Like one of the guys.

Offense lined up. Coach blew his whistle. Kevin, not just their best runner but the fastest kid on the team by a lot, took a pitch from Jarrod Benedict on first down, got to the edge in a blink, looked as if he might end the scrimmage on one play before Kyle Nichols, one of their safeties, came flying in to knock him out of bounds after a ten-yard gain.

On second down the tight end, Billy Gallo, caught a short pass in front of Charlie, Charlie having no chance to break it up, but managing to drive a shoulder into Billy and slow him down before Kyle came from the backside again to put him down for real.

Ball on the ten now, two downs left.

The offense ran Kevin again, same toss. This time he ran for eight yards, cutting back when he saw some daylight, finally brought down at the two by a swarm of defenders.

Last play.

Either the offense would score and get to watch the defense run, or the other way around.

In their huddle Kyle Nichols said, "No way I'm running more than I already have today."

"Then you better get one more stop, big boy," Coach Fallon said.

Charlie could feel his heart trying to get out of his chest, not wanting to be the one who messed up and made the rest of the guys on D have to run. It was funny, Charlie thought, when you were in the game and in the moment, when it was happening to *you*, even in Pop Warner and even in practice, everything seemed to speed up.

No DVR out here; you couldn't stop things, replay them as much as you wanted, sometimes just to confirm what your eyes told you when you'd watched a play in real time.

The offense lined up. Billy Gallo on Charlie's side of the field again. As soon as Billy took his stance, before Jarrod starting calling signals, Charlie took a deep breath, looked over to Coach Fallon on the sideline, and yelled over to him.

"Are we allowed to call a time-out?"

"Excuse me?"

"Coach, can we call a time-out like we would in a real game?"

Coach Fallon made a gesture with his hands, palms up, his way of saying he had no idea, looked over at Coach Dayley and said, "Little help here, Ed?"

Coach Dayley told the guys on offense to hold on, came jogging over to Charlie. Grin on his face.

"It's Charlie, right?"

"Yes, sir. Charlie Gaines."

"The one they call Brain."

Charlie said, "It's more of a joke than anything else, Coach."

"So why do you want to call time, Charlie?"

Charlie took another deep breath and in a low voice said to his coach, "I know . . . I *think* I know what they're going to run. Well, actually, what *you're* going to run, Coach."

"Do you now?"

"Yes, sir."

"Care to tell me?"

Charlie tipped back his helmet now so Coach could see him grinning as he said, "You promise you won't tell?"

"Promise," he said. "But I'm not going to tell you if you're right, either."

"Fair enough."

"What you got?"

"You're going to throw to Billy again."

"And you know this . . . *how*?"

"The two plays when you ran the ball," Charlie said, still keeping his voice low, "Billy lined up practically shoulder to shoulder with the tackle. But when he was going to be the receiver, he put more space between him and the tackle. And I noticed this time he put down his outside hand when he took his stance, the way he did when he caught that ball in front of me. I think it helps him make a quicker move off the line."

Coach Dayley started to say something but before he did, Charlie said, "Plus, I'm thinking that if you ran the same pitch play twice, you'll do the same with that short pass, since it worked the first time."

Coach Dayley just stared at him.

Finally he said, "That all?"

"Pretty much."

"Call your time-out. If you're right, and I'm not saying you are, I promise not to change the play. Then we'll just snap the ball and see how it all turns out."

Charlie turned to his defensive teammates, as if this were a real game, raised his arms, brought his hands together, fingers into palm, signaling time-out. They huddled up again. He told them what he'd seen, what he thought they were going to run. Told Kyle Nichols that he couldn't cover Billy Gallo on a bet, and to pinch in so he was there as soon as the ball was snapped and Jarrod took the same quick drop he had before.

"I explained I didn't want to run laps," Kyle said to Charlie. "You heard that, right?"

Charlie nodded.

"You really got this?" Kyle said.

Charlie Gaines—Brain—said, "I do."

Billy Gallo lined up where he had before. Same way he had before. A good yard of separation this time between him and the tackle. Outside hand down.

Charlie moved up a little, knowing that they needed just two yards for a score. Knowing that if Jarrod made a good throw once Billy made his quick move to the outside, it was all over, easy score.

Jarrod went to a quick count, took his quick drop. Billy was turning his body as he came off the line, putting his inside shoulder past Charlie with no problem, like Charlie was nothing more than a speed bump.

For one split second, Billy looked to be wide open again.

Until he wasn't.

Until Kyle Nichols, having snuck in behind the middle

linebacker, flying again as soon as the ball was snapped, launched himself between the ball and Billy, left arm outstretched, knocked the ball to the ground.

The guys on the defense whooped and high-fived each other as if they'd just won the first game of the season, not just the first day of practice.

Charlie hadn't made the play himself, but felt as if he at least ought to get an assist.

Kyle Nichols came over, helmet already in his hand, slapped Charlie hard on his left shoulder pad. Then did it again.

"You really saw all that in three plays?"

"Kind of."

Kyle shook his head.

"Brain," he said, grinning. "I could definitely use one of those."

Now Coach Dayley and Coach Fallon were both walking toward Charlie.

Coach Dayley said, "That was pretty cool, I have to say."

"My friends on offense won't be too happy with me," Charlie said.

They were running the first of two long laps around the entire field.

"They'll get over it," Coach said. "Important thing is, *I'm* happy with you."

"Why?"

"Because I just found myself the first player-coach in the history of Culver City Pop Warner," he said.

"I take it that would be me?" Charlie said.

"Wow," Coach Dayley said. "They really don't call you Brain for nothing."

He put his arm around Charlie. "But listen to me," he said. "Just because I'm calling you my assistant, I still think of you as a player, okay?"

"Okay."

"And just because there are guys ahead of you at outside line-backer doesn't mean you should stop trying to prove me wrong and earn yourself more playing time."

"I don't think you're wrong about me, Coach," Charlie said. "But I won't stop trying."

Then Coach Ed Dayley said, "I don't know how much you're going to end up playing this season, kid. But I've got this feeling you're going to make a contribution."

Charlie hoping it would be doing something more than doing what he was doing right now: standing next to his coach.

Five

BULLDOGS VS. ST. LOUIS RAMS the next Saturday night, Charlie and Anna in her grandfather's suite, about an hour before kickoff.

Anna said, "It used to be more crowded in here the first couple of seasons, even during the preseason. You could see a lot of celebrities doing what they do best: being seen."

"Like actors at Lakers games," Charlie said.

Anna nodded.

"Now I think the ones who show up do their best acting when they act as if they really want to be here," she said.

"Some of them must be real fans."

"Some of them are. But it's like my dad says about Hollywood people: Nobody fakes sincerity better than they do." She made a snorting sound. "Sometimes I see them smiling and waving when the cameras are on them, especially the ones sitting next to my gramps, and want to gag."

"Hey," Charlie said, "I thought we agreed we were going to have a positive attitude tonight about our team and everything else? Your mom said if we act happy it will make your grandfather happy."

Anna stared across the room now at Joe Warren. "I want him to be happy more than anything else in the world."

It was hard for Charlie to think that Mr. Warren, the owner of the team—*Charlie's* team—was anybody's gramps, even if the people writing about him and talking about him and the team the way they did on the radio always went out of their way to point out what a gentleman he was. Then they'd hammer away at him again, blaming him for the state of the team, saying that nothing would change until he made the changes he needed to make in the front office, which meant firing his son, Matt.

Kevin Fallon's dad was usually the one leading the charge on his talk show on L.A.'s ESPN station, having taken to calling the Bulldogs' general manager "Door-Matt" Warren.

Somehow, in some people's eyes, Anna's gramps had gone from being a local hero for bringing football back, to being some out-of-it old geezer who acted as if he didn't care whether the Bulldogs won or lost.

"Anybody who thinks he doesn't care," Anna had said on the ride to the game from Culver City, "is dumber than all of the Kardashian sisters combined."

Charlie had said, "They make a lot of money for dumb people, though, don't they?"

"Shut up."

Charlie watched Joe Warren greet each new guest as they

came through the door to the suite. He was tall and white-haired, wearing a white shirt, a blue-striped tie, and the same blazer he always seemed to be wearing when you'd see him being interviewed on television. And no matter how tough the questions that were being shouted at him—the reporters acting as if the Bulldogs' record was happening to them, making them angry—Joe Warren would smile and answer all of them politely and never lose his temper.

He reminded Charlie more of some nice old teacher or minister than the loud owners of some of the other teams—the guys who acted like they were bigger stars than their own players.

"Let's go rescue him," Anna said now.

"He seems to be pretty busy being a good host."

She grinned at him. "Gramps is *never* too busy for his precious princess."

"He calls you that?"

"Got a problem?" Anna grabbed Charlie by the arm and the two of them made their way across the suite.

"How's the world's handsomest grandfather?" Anna said when they got to him.

"Better now that you're here," he said. "We have a beautiful night for football and I've got the most beautiful girl on the planet standing next to me, lying about my looks."

He noticed Charlie now. "How's the biggest Bulldogs fan doing?"

"Hey!" Anna said.

"Apologies," Joe Warren said. "What I meant to say is, how's the biggest *boy* Bulldogs fan doing?"

"Excited to be here," Charlie said, shaking his hand and looking him in the eye, the way his mother had taught him.

"You'll sit on one side of me when the game starts," Joe Warren said, "and Anna will be on the other. Unless you can find a better date in the next forty-five minutes or so."

"He couldn't find one in forty-five years."

"Do you ever want to mute this young lady the way you do a television set?" Joe Warren said.

"You have no idea," Charlie said.

"The two of *you* have no idea," Anna said, "how lucky you both are to have me."

"She makes it sound as if we're in a special club, doesn't she, Charlie boy?" Joe Warren said.

"Only because she believes it," Charlie said to him.

Charlie watched Anna's grandfather shuffle off to greet more guests now. He hadn't seen him since the last game of last season, and noticed how much older he looked now than he had then, how much slower he seemed to be moving.

"Such a good guy," Charlie said.

"The best," Anna said, watching her grandfather smile and take a woman's hand and kiss it.

The woman said something to Joe Warren. He laughed.

"How old is he?" Charlie said.

"Seventy-nine, but he doesn't think old and he doesn't act old.

He still thinks every day is going to be the best day of his whole life."

Charlie thought Anna's eyes were starting to fill up as she said, "My mom always says that God likes Gramps best. But every time she says that, I ask her if that's true, how come He won't give him a better football team?"

Six

"TRUE STORY," JOE WARREN WAS saying to Charlie and Anna now.

Charlie on his right, Anna on his left. Not a bad game so far, even for the preseason. Not many mistakes, three good drives, and the Bulldogs ahead 14–7 halfway through the second quarter. JJ Guerrero was in at quarterback for Chase Sisk by now, moving the team a lot better than Chase had before his night was over.

"You start out every story by saying 'true story,'" Anna said.

Joe Warren looked at Charlie. "I assume she's this much of a know-it-all with you?"

"She doesn't think her family name is Warren, sir," Charlie said. "She thinks it's Google."

"You should start out by saying 'good story,'" Anna said. "Because they always are, Gramps."

Joe Warren rubbed the back of her head.

"See those horns on the side of the Rams' helmets," the old man said. "A Rams player back in the day, back when I was a boy, painted horns on his helmet one day in 1948. And people liked the way it looked so much that it became the first team emblem on a helmet in the whole league."

Even Charlie hadn't known that.

Down on the field JJ Guerrero scrambled to his right, pulled up, threw a little floater to the tight end for a first down.

"He makes better decisions than Chase Sisk," Joe Warren said.

"Chase thinks that because he's got a cannon for an arm," Charlie said, "he can throw it into any kind of coverage."

"I wish he'd just throw it away sometimes rather than try to force it in there," Joe Warren said.

Charlie said, "I read this quote once about how smart football coaches graded quarterbacks the way basketball coaches graded point guards. He said the only stat he cared about was the final score, and whether they'd scored more points than the other team."

Joe Warren turned to Anna and said, "I forgot from last season to this one how much football this boy really knows."

"See, Gramps," she said. "He's the one who's a know-it-all, not me."

Joe Warren turned back to Charlie now. "Bet you didn't know that we used to have two pro teams in L.A. when I was a boy."

"Rams and Dons," Charlie said. "Before they merged into one team."

Anna's gramps made a whistling sound.

Charlie shrugged. "I can't help it, Mr. Warren. History's my favorite subject in school, and football is my favorite subject, period."

"Okay, one more trivia question: The old Rams moved here from somewhere else. What city was it?"

"Cleveland."

And Joe Warren threw up his hands. "I give up."

Now JJ Guerrero was the one forcing a throw, trying to complete a deep out pattern that Charlie knew was too much for his arm, getting intercepted at the Rams' twenty-two-yard line.

"Look at that, Gramps!" Anna said. "Same old same old."

"I've been saying we need a veteran quarterback to play behind Chase and work with him," the old man said. "Or just to get us to the next kid who'll hopefully turn out to be what we hoped Chase would be."

As the Bulldogs' defense came back on the field, Anna reached behind her grandfather and pinched Charlie's arm.

"Ow?" he said.

"Tell Gramps what you were saying last night about Tom Pinkett," Anna said.

Charlie shook his head, no. Eyes pleading with her to drop this.

"Tell me what?" Joe Warren said.

"Tell him what or I will," Anna said.

"Your grandfather doesn't want to hear what I think about an old guy the Bengals are probably going to cut," Charlie said. "And you know I talk just to talk sometimes."

"Actually," Anna said, "you never do that."

"What *about* Tom Pinkett?" Joe Warren said. "I forgot he was even still in the league."

Charlie, talking too fast, told him what he thought. He said that the Bengals had brought in three veteran quarterbacks to see which one of them would be best to back up their starter, who hadn't missed a start in four seasons. Even if Tom Pinkett made the team, he'd be nothing more than an insurance policy.

But watching a few minutes of highlights the night before, Charlie thought he had shown way more arm than the last time he had really gotten a chance to play, two years ago with the Dolphins.

"So you're a fan of his?" Joe Warren said. "The last time Tom was even close to being a star in this league was before you were born."

"Just going off what I saw."

"You seem to have seen plenty."

"Just paying attention, Mr. Warren."

The Rams ran out the clock on the rest of the half. Joe Warren stood up. "More meeting and greeting?" Anna said.

"No," her grandfather said, sounding tired all of a sudden. "If I don't get up and move around, my back has a tendency to stiffen up."

He left them there.

"He really likes you," Anna said.

"He's *being* nice to me, there's a difference."

"Nope. He means it with you the way he means it with me."

When the second half started Joe Warren was back with them, saying that he didn't hate many things in the world but small talk was one of them.

Then the three of them went back to watching the game as if it really mattered, maybe because it did to them, even if it was mostly being played now by rookies and free agents and veterans trying to show the coaches enough to make it through the next round of cuts at the end of the week.

Mr. Warren seemed to say less and look more tired as the game wore on. But he still didn't miss much. They talked a lot about Michael Gilmore, Charlie saying he didn't just like the guy, he loved him. Joe Warren agreed, so Charlie leaned back in his chair and shot Anna an I-told-you-so look. Charlie told Mr. Warren that the only mistake the Bulldogs would make was if they thought of him as a speed guy on the outside.

"He can catch in traffic," Charlie said. "And he's not afraid to go over the middle of the field."

Gilmore was in the game now, having caught three balls from JJ Guerrero on the current drive, one of them when he was lined up in the slot, which is where Charlie was sure he belonged.

"Your friend definitely isn't shy," Mr. Warren said to Anna.

"Actually, Gramps," she said, "the funny thing is that he *is*. Just not when a football game breaks out."

Charlie was locked in on Gilmore now, studying his every move. The next play was an innocent-looking curl pattern, Gilmore spinning away from the linebacker toward the sideline. There was a lot of green in front of him. Gilmore stopped his spin move, planted his leg, and tried to push off.

That's when he went down. Untouched. Right leg buckling underneath him as he tried to cut back to the inside.

Charlie knew: Sometimes the worst injuries were the ones like this, nobody laying a hand on the guy.

Michael Gilmore was rolling around on the ground now, in obvious pain, holding his knee.

"Get up," Charlie said in a soft voice. "Please get up."

"Nothing happened to make him go down," Anna said.

"Sometimes," Charlie said in the same soft voice, "it means everything just happened."

Before long, the team's trainers lifted Michael Gilmore up and carefully sat him on the flatbed back of the golf cart, and the people cheered and Gilmore waved once before he disappeared into the tunnel.

Charlie and Anna and Joe Warren stood and cheered along with everybody else, then Charlie excused himself and went to the bathroom and closed the door behind him and locked it. Looked into the mirror and saw the red eyes he didn't want anybody else to see.

Thinking that Anna was right about something, more than she knew.

"Crazy fan," he said to himself.

Even though the night had changed, he was still here, still with Anna and her gramps, determined not to let Michael Gilmore's injury ruin the fact that he was sitting here with them, in Mr. Warren's suite.

Especially when a real game broke out in the fourth quarter, with all the third- and fourth-stringers on the field. Finally it was 24–24 in the last minute, the Rams were pinned back on their two-yard line, but still giving one of their rookie quarterbacks a chance to win.

First down, two time-outs left, a chance for the Rams to move into field-goal range if they could pick up a couple of long first downs. The rookie quarterback, Kevin Mahoney, lined up in the shotgun, halfway back in the end zone.

Mahoney took the snap, rolled to his right.

Charlie saw Cliff McFeely, rookie outside linebacker, coming from the quarterback's blind side, knowing Mahoney sure didn't see him.

The Rams' running back, who was supposed to be covering for his quarterback, saw McFeely, too. And rather than give up a sack, and a sure safety, the running back's solution was to do this:

Not just wrap up Cliff McFeely before he could sack the St. Louis quarterback, but tackle him.

"We win," Charlie said, almost like he was talking to himself, even before the referee's flag hit the ground for the holding penalty he was about to call.

"We win?" Joe Warren said.

"He thought he was preventing a safety," Charlie said. "But the Rams are gonna get called for one anyway. Offensive holding in the end zone is a safety." He shrugged. "Guess the guy didn't know the rules."

First the ref signaled holding, then he signaled safety, putting his hands on top of his head.

Mr. Warren high-fived Anna and then Charlie, saying, "We do win!"

Then he looked at Charlie and said, "That poor running back didn't know that rule. But *you* did."

"Doesn't everybody know the rules?" Charlie said.

When the game was over, Bulldogs winning 26–24, Anna's mom and dad came over and said they were going to wait awhile for the traffic to thin out, Mrs. Bretton adding, "Of course in L.A. that can mean waiting until the Pacific Ocean dries up."

Charlie and Anna sat in a quiet corner of the suite where there was a bank of televisions and watched highlights of the rest of the preseason games played that night. And watched as well Michael Gilmore's injury replayed until Charlie couldn't watch it one more time. Anna finally said she was hungry again.

"When are you *not* hungry?" Charlie asked.

"When the Bulldogs make me lose my appetite," she said. "Fortunately that wasn't the case tonight." She went off to make herself a sundae at the ice cream bar near the buffet table.

Charlie went back outside, sat where he had been sitting with Mr. Warren and Anna, and watched the night come to an end, some of the lights, but not all, being switched off at the top of Bulldogs Stadium. Knowing this was part of it, part of being a crazy fan, experiencing the joy of the way the game had ended right after he had seen Michael Gilmore get hurt the way he did.

On the field, he saw JJ Guerrero come walking across, holding the hand of a little boy who had to be his son, the boy looking to be about half Charlie's age. Saw the boy break away from his dad, run toward the nearest end zone, suddenly dive across the goal line.

JJ Guerrero dropped his bag, jogged after him, picked him up, and held him over his head like a trophy.

All night long Charlie had thought how lucky he was to watch the game from up here.

Not nearly as lucky as JJ Guerrero's son, his dad holding him high in the sky.

Behind him he heard Joe Warren say, "When the game's over, I like to do exactly what you're doing."

The old man lowered himself down into his seat. "Like I'm putting the place to bed."

Just the two of them out here.

Me and the owner of the L.A. Bulldogs, Charlie thought.

Hangin'.

"Thank you so much again for inviting me, Mr. Warren," Charlie said. "I had the best time tonight."

"My pleasure, Charlie. And I will call Anna tomorrow when I find out more about your man Gilmore, and have her call you," he said.

"Thank you, sir."

"Even with that," Joe Warren said, "I think people went home happy tonight, didn't they?"

"They did."

"Wish it happened more often."

"Someday it will," Charlie said, mostly because he wanted that to be true.

"Will it, Charlie boy?"

"Maybe it will just take more time than you thought it would."

"Time," the old man said, staring out at the field.

They were silent for a few minutes, both of them seeming comfortable with that. The music that had been playing over the loudspeaker was turned off. Joe Warren turned to Charlie and said, "I am going to tell my granddaughter that you have a standing invitation to home games this season."

"You'd better *ask* her," Charlie said, grinning at him. "Not only does Anna act like she runs the family, I think her ultimate goal is world domination."

"But I still run the Bulldogs." Joe Warren turned to Charlie, put out his hand, and added, "Deal?"

"Deal," Charlie said, shaking his hand, surprised at how weak his grip was, how cold his hand felt. Maybe it was an old-person thing.

"The way you look at our team is the way I want everybody to look at it," Joe Warren said.

"In sports, your team is your team," Charlie said. "The Bulldogs are mine."

"Mine, too," the old man said. "Mine, too, Charlie."

Four days later the Bengals released Tom Pinkett and the Bulldogs signed him.

Seven

THE PODCAST WAS ANNA'S IDEA.

"You're a natural," Anna said to Charlie.

"And you're insane," he said.

"No, I'm right, as usual," she said. "You'd be a natural talking about football."

"I'm good talking about football in front of you," Charlie said.

"What about Gramps?" Anna said. "Not only are the two of you practically boys now, he thought enough of what you were saying that he went out and signed Tom Pinkett."

"First of all," Charlie said, "I'm sure the Bulldogs' scouts must have approved of him, too."

"Keep telling yourself that."

"And second of all," Charlie said, "you know better than anybody that I don't even like to get up in front of the class when I have to speak."

"But see, that's the beauty of doing a podcast," she said. "You don't have to look at anybody when you're talking to them. You just talk to me."

He said that he didn't know anything about doing a podcast.

Anna said, "I do."

Of course she did. Of course she would. Charlie knew it was part of the fun of knowing her, being inside what Charlie's mom called Anna's force field. She wasn't just a jock. She was a huge techie, too. Sometimes something would go wrong with one of the computers at Anna's house when her dad wasn't around, and Anna's mom would call up to her and ask her to fix it.

She loved gadgets the way she loved social networking and Instagram and all the rest of it. And if some new gadget came along or was even in the chute, she was the one at school who knew about it first.

So now in Charlie's room, she was talking about multimedia posts, blogs, streaming, audio files, free hosting, and something called Soundsnap for intro music.

"Intro music?" Charlie said. "Now I've got my own theme music?"

"Just throwing it out there," she said.

"Yeah," he said. "But sometimes when you throw stuff out there, I'm the one who needs to duck."

"You'll sound smarter than half the guys on Kevin's dad's station," she said. "Not only should most of those guys not be allowed to talk on the radio, they shouldn't be allowed to talk, period."

Charlie looked at Anna, sitting there cross-legged on his bed, looking happy and excited. She'd said her grandfather thought every day was going to be the best of his whole life. Now Charlie knew where Anna got it from.

Or maybe he got it from her.

"You never mentioned a podcast before," he said. "Now you act as if I'm insane if I don't do it."

"Not only are you going to do it," she said. "But I'm going to produce it."

"Now you're a *producer*?"

She nodded. "Yup. This is going to be *huge*. Wait till people hear how much a twelve-year-old kid from Culver City knows about the Bulldogs and the rest of pro football."

"It *would* be kind of cool having a show," Charlie said. "I wouldn't be one more guy on the radio hating on our team."

He turned and saw Anna smiling at him.

"This is L.A.," she said. "You know what they say here."

"What do they say here?" Charlie said.

"Kid, I'm gonna make you a star."

And that is how *The Charlie Show* was born.

Eight

ANNA SAID THAT ALL CHARLIE had to do was think of *The Charlie Show* as his own personal diary, just with him saying what was on his mind instead of writing it down.

"I don't write in a diary, either, not that you asked," he said. "And no one would want to read it if I did."

He and Anna were in his room, sitting on the floor, all set up with his new microphone and headphones, and GarageBand installed on his laptop to do their first podcast.

"That's where you're wrong, Sparky," she said.

"I hate when you call me that, have I mentioned that to you?" he said. "Sparky sounds like a puppy."

"You hating it is why I do it, silly," she said, making that sound like the most obvious thing in the world. "Besides, you know how much other kids bug you for your fantasy picks? Now everybody is going to want them."

"Everybody," he said. "You make it sound like we're going to have a bigger audience than one of those singing shows."

"I always thought you should be putting your picks out there," she said. "You know as much as the guys on the fantasy football shows on TV."

"I like sharing picks with you, not strangers."

"Don't worry," Anna said. "You will."

Their parents, all of whom loved the idea of the podcast—Anna's mom even suggested they should try to get school credits for it—helped with the cost of a real radio microphone and brand-new headsets. For the past few days, Anna had been trying to explain the process of a podcast to Charlie, but to him it was the same as if she were trying to explain how to take his laptop apart and put it back together.

They had already done some practice episodes and played them back, listened to them. Anna graded them like a hard teacher grading papers. But they had been good enough that Anna had now started promoting *The Charlie Show* on her Facebook page, even counting down the days to it.

Some of the practice episodes had been with Charlie alone, some with him talking to her once in a while. Finally Anna had decided—who else was going to decide?—that on the first official episode the only voice anybody would hear would be Charlie's.

"It's the world premiere!" she said. "We've got to make sure they know who the star of the show is."

"Yeah," he said. "All eight people who will be listening."

"I don't need any of your attitude, mister," she said.

"But if I ask you to talk, you will, right?"

Anna said, "I guess I could say a few words, if asked nicely."

She said that because it was still the preseason, one more game before Week One of the regular season. This would be a good chance for them to really see what worked on the show and what didn't. They had agreed that the first part of the show would deal with the Bulldogs, looking back at last week's game and ahead to the next one. The second part would just be stuff from around the league that Charlie found interesting, his opinions about the biggest games and biggest stories of the previous week.

The last part of the show—Anna described it as "wait for it, I'm Charlie and I'm awesome"—would be Charlie talking fantasy football, including some of the picks he expected to make for the regular season.

"Once people figure out how good you are at this, it's going to be *huge*," she said. "Thing could go viral by the second week. Now relax. Just pretend you're talking to me and have fun."

"Who said talking to you is fun?"

She gave a whoop of laughter and punched him in the arm, did a check of the microphone, put her fist back out but just to get some pound from him this time.

"Let's do this," she said.

And they did, Charlie pretending he was hosting one of those pro football shows on ESPN. Except he was hosting it from his room. Anna had said they could take breaks if they wanted to, and they did after the first segment, Charlie saying he thought he wanted to have her voice in the segment as they went around the league, maybe setting him up with questions.

At one point she asked him what he thought about fans and the media hating on the Bulldogs the way they did, especially since

L.A. had waited twenty years for a team after the Rams had left. Not saying who she was, not saying who her grandfather and uncle were.

She called herself "Football Girl."

Charlie said: "I know people are always talking about how great the weather is in L.A. Maybe that's why we seem to have more fair-weather fans than any other place in America."

Anna gave him a fist pump on that one.

Then he talked a little about Tom Pinkett, how happy he was to have him on the Bulldogs, not saying he was the one who'd told Joe Warren about Pinkett when Pinkett was still on the bench in Cincinnati. He and Anna had agreed that would remain their secret.

"That's all we'd need," Anna had said, "people thinking Gramps is getting advice from a twelve-year-old."

Before long Charlie was going through some of the fantasy picks he expected to make in the early rounds of his drafts, which defenses he had his eye on. Then it was over, Charlie amazed at how fast the time had gone, Anna telling him the show had timed out at just under thirty minutes.

The last thing he'd done was talk about some surprise fantasy picks he might have for the opening week of the season.

"But if you want to find out what those surprises are," he said, "you really are going to have to tune in to the next *Charlie Show.*"

Anna grabbed the microphone back at that point, like even on his show *she* had to get the last word in.

"Think of missing a show like missing a class," she said. "One that's going to be taught by the Fantasy King."

"So says Football Girl, who thinks she's a queen," Charlie said. "Talk to you next week, everybody."

They had done the show sitting on the floor of Charlie's room, his laptop between them. Anna closed the laptop now. Took off her headset. Charlie did the same. They stared at each other for a moment, neither one of them saying anything. Then Anna Bretton high-fived Charlie so hard she nearly knocked him over on his back.

"Huge!" she said.

Nine

THE CULVER CITY CARDINALS PLAYED their opener against the Venice Bears the day before the Bulldogs were going to open their season at home against the 49ers.

Jarrod Benedict threw for one touchdown and Kevin Fallon ran for another while Venice only crossed midfield twice in the whole game—the Cardinals' defense was that good. Charlie played on both the kickoff and punt teams, got some good plays in at outside linebacker for the last two minutes, and even knocked down a pass intended for Venice's big tight end on the second-to-last play of the game.

He spent the rest of the day at Memorial Field thinking of himself as an assistant coach, standing next to Coach Dayley. He had even identified a couple of Venice blitzes before they happened, so sure that one blitz was coming from Jarrod's blind side that Coach Dayley ran out on the field before the ball was snapped and asked for a time-out.

Coach changed the pass play he'd called to a draw, Venice stayed in the same defense, and Kevin Fallon ran straight up the middle, blowing past the attacking Venice defense. He ended up gaining twenty yards.

"Kid," Coach Dayley said after the play, "you see things on the field that make me think I ought to have my sunglasses checked." Then before Charlie could say anything Coach put a hand on his arm, stopping him before he started, and said, "I know, I know, you're just paying attention."

"It's true," Charlie said.

"Everybody pays attention, Charlie. Your paying attention is just a little different."

It was a good day. The team won and Charlie made a couple of good calls for Coach. And he got to play. He could be Brain the rest of the week. He could be the boy Fantasy King. In that world, he did feel like the star of the team. *All* his fantasy teams. There he could throw like Jarrod and run the way Kevin Fallon did. But in his heart he knew something:

On Saturdays, the thing he wanted the most was to go home with a dirty uniform.

A dirty uniform made him feel like a real player, even if he had probably done more to help his team standing next to Coach than he had on the field.

Normally playing a game like this and winning it would have felt like the best part of his Saturday, even before he and Anna and Kevin went into town, maybe had lunch at Wildcraft Pizza and then went over to the Coolhaus Shop, which used to just be a fancy truck, for ice cream.

Just not this Saturday.

This Saturday his mom was driving him home and he was going to take a shower and put on a polo shirt to go with his good shorts before she drove him to Anna's house. After that Anna's mom was going to drive them over to Joe Warren's house in Bel Air for lunch.

"I *told* you," Anna had said to him on Friday at school, telling him about the invitation to have lunch with her and her grandfather. "You and Gramps really are boys now!"

Charlie already knew that even though Anna's grandmother had died when she was in the first grade, Joe Warren still lived in the same big house a couple of blocks from the Hotel Bel-Air.

Anna had told Charlie that her Gramps wasn't alone in the house; there was a couple, husband and wife, who lived in a small cottage on the property. The wife cleaned and cooked for Anna's grandfather. The husband drove him around and tended to the grounds, which Anna said required a whole lot of tending, wait until Charlie saw them.

"Gramps giving up driving himself around was a big thing," Anna said. "But it had just turned into bumper cars for him."

"*Anna,*" her mom said from the front seat of the car as they headed toward Bel Air, "your grandfather just had a couple of little fender benders."

"*Mom,*" Anna said, trying to imitate her mother's tone. "One time he hit a mailbox and a tree coming out of his own driveway. Dad said if he'd clipped the doors to the gate and the fire hydrant by the street, it would have given him a grand slam."

There was a huge iron gate at the entrance to the driveway, one that didn't open automatically. Anna's mom had to punch in a code. Then they drove up a steep hill, past more old, thick trees than Charlie thought he'd ever seen.

Like everything on the property was as old as Joe Warren was.

He was waiting for them when they got to the top of the drive, wearing a light green sweater, khaki pants with a sharp crease in them, and loafers without socks.

"Look at you, Gramps," Anna said, jumping out of the car and running to hug him, "you look like a movie producer."

"That, young lady, is a very mean thing to say to a senior citizen," he said, kissing the top of her head. "Or any citizen, for that matter."

He turned to Charlie and said, "Well, hello, Mr. Gaines."

Charlie nodded respectfully. "Mr. Warren."

"Anna told me on the phone that your team got its first win this morning."

"Two tackles for him," Anna said. "The college scouts will be coming around any day."

"She's just making stuff up," Charlie said.

Anna said, "Not about the two tackles."

Charlie looked at Joe Warren and said, "Played special teams and got in at garbage time, is all."

"You played, you won, it's a beautiful day in the City of Angels," Joe Warren said. "I believe I'd much rather be you—and be your age today—than me."

Anna's mom said she was going shopping in Brentwood and

would be back in a few hours. Joe Warren told her to take as much time she wanted. Then he walked Charlie and Anna through the front door, through a living room that Charlie thought was about half as long as a football field, a den filled with bookcases that stretched all the way to the ceiling and the biggest television screen Charlie had ever seen outside a stadium, through a huge kitchen and out to the back patio. There stood a lawn that was *longer* than a football field, Charlie was sure, the grass amazingly green and perfect. Of course there were more big old trees back here, like they were trying to block out the rest of the world.

Charlie immediately noticed how still it was back here, the chirping of birds the only sound, Charlie thinking even the birds were keeping their voices down. The three of them sat down and an older woman Joe Warren called Maria brought a pitcher of iced tea with three glasses, Maria telling them that lunch would be served in about twenty minutes, if that was all right with them.

"Your lunches are always worth waiting for, Maria," Anna's grandfather said.

When she was gone Joe Warren turned to Charlie and said, "Got a little football news that even you don't have yet."

"Oh," Anna said, "so it's only news for *him*? Let me remind you of something, Gramps. I can talk with the best of 'em."

"No kidding," Charlie said.

He saw her smiling at her grandfather.

Joe Warren said, "It just happens to be news that will mean more to Charlie. About our team."

Our team. As if it suddenly belonged to all of them.

Charlie and Anna waited until the old man said, "Your quarterback is starting tomorrow against the 49ers. Our coach is probably telling the media that right now over at the stadium."

"My quarterback?" Charlie said.

"Tom Pinkett."

"You're joking."

"While there are many in the Los Angeles area who believe our entire quarterbacking situation is a joke," the old man said, "I am certainly not joking. Your man Pinkett is under center tomorrow afternoon at one."

Chase Sisk, as all Bulldogs fans knew by then, had sprained his shoulder the previous Saturday night against the Saints after taking a hard sack. Officially he was listed as doubtful for the season opener, but everyone knew there was no way the team was going to risk losing him for the season by rushing him back.

Charlie felt bad for the guy. He'd been allowed to go down to the locker room for a few minutes after the Rams game, and Chase had been as nice as any of the players he'd been introduced to. But Charlie the football guy, Brain, knew Sisk's injury wasn't a bad thing for the Bulldogs, just because he never thought Chase Sisk was ever going to be anything more than a big arm with a much smaller football brain.

Not that he ever would have said that to Anna's grandfather.

But once Chase was gone, Charlie had just assumed that JJ Guerrero, his backup, would move up and be given a chance to show what he could do. Charlie and everybody else in town. Until now.

Joe Warren picked up his glass, Charlie noticing the tremor in his hand, afraid he was going to spill some of his drink. But he just gestured for Charlie to pick up his.

They touched glasses.

"Cheers," Joe Warren said. "And thanks, kiddo."

"For what?"

He took a sip of his iced tea. Maria's was way better than Snapple.

"We never would have signed him if you hadn't said something to me that night," Joe Warren said.

Then he winked at Charlie, smiled and said, "True story."

When lunch was over Anna said she was going inside to watch some of the USC game on television. They were playing one of the early-season college football games against Florida.

"You're even watching *college* football now?" her grandfather said.

"She thinks the Trojans' sophomore quarterback is cuter than all of her boy bands put together," Charlie said.

"See *you* in a few," she said to Joe Warren, kissing him on the cheek. "And you shut up, Charlie Gaines."

When she was gone, Joe Warren said to Charlie, "C'mon, I'll show you my really quiet place."

It took some effort for him to get out of his chair, and Charlie almost jumped up to give him a hand. But the old man made it, and pointed down to the end of the lawn.

"Down there," Joe Warren said, and began walking slowly

down the hill, in that careful walk you saw from old people, making sure not to shuffle his feet, picking them up and placing them on the grass in front of him, as if the next step he was going to take might be the one that put him down.

Anna had told Charlie on the way over that her grandfather refused to use a cane, even though the rest of the family thought he needed one.

The lawn went slightly downhill, down toward the last clump of trees. But then there was a path through them, and they walked into this beautiful, tiny garden, Charlie and Joe Warren standing in the middle of all these bright, amazing colors.

Joe Warren, Charlie could see, was so tired it was as if he had just walked up a hill, face red, out of breath.

"Sorry it took so long to get here," Joe Warren said. "But my late friend Red Auerbach, who built the Boston Celtics, once gave me just two words of advice about growing older. Would you like to know what those two words are?"

"I would."

"Don't fall," Joe Warren said, and then lowered himself into one of the two cushioned chairs positioned perfectly to catch the sun at this time of day.

He smiled at Charlie now. "An old actress friend of mine once said that getting old ain't for sissies. But you have to get as old as I am to find out how true that really is."

Then he told Charlie how he and his wife used to come out here at the end of the day, sometimes before dinner and sometimes afterward. And how he still liked to come down here when the sun was setting and talk to her for a few minutes the way he always had before she was gone.

"I even used to put on some music and dance with her down here, Charlie. Sometimes I still do that, too." He smiled at Charlie. "I keep telling myself that one of these days I might kick up my heels and dance at the stadium if this team of mine ever makes it into the playoffs."

"She sounds pretty special," Charlie said. "Mrs. Warren, I mean."

"She was the one who always told me the truth," Joe Warren said. "Still does, as a matter of fact."

Charlie thought it was weird, the idea of talking to dead people. But the old man looked happy just talking about it.

"She was never *afraid* to tell me the truth," he said. "Never afraid to tell me things she thought I needed to hear even if I didn't want to hear them sometimes."

He paused, put his head back to take in some sun.

"Now I seem to have surrounded myself with people who won't tell me the truth. Or just give a version they think the poor old guy can handle."

He turned and looked hard at Charlie, Charlie thinking Joe Warren's blue eyes were the youngest part of him. The brightest.

"You're a smart kid, Charlie," he said. "You must know where I'm going with this."

"It's about your team."

"I love my son, don't get me wrong," Joe Warren said. "And he loves me. And we're going to build the Bulldogs into a champion together, I believe that in my heart. In the process, we were also going to finally have the father-son time we didn't nearly have enough of when he was growing up."

Whatever it was, it was more than I had, Charlie thought.

"But now the whole thing is a mess, despite my best intentions. And his . . ." His voice trailed off, running out of steam. "When I made the suggestion to him about Tom Pinkett, he acted as if I didn't trust his judgment anymore. Said that I had installed him as general manager so he could make football decisions. Then I got my back up a little and said that in addition to being the owner of the team, I was also team president last time I checked."

Charlie waited.

"He said that any time I wanted to replace him, I should go ahead. I told him that I had done a little research and felt that Tom Pinkett might be a better backup than JJ, might even turn out to be our best option at quarterback this season. And lo and behold? Our coach ended up agreeing with me."

Charlie didn't know what to say, so they sat there in silence for a few minutes, Joe Warren tipping his head back again to let the sun hit his face.

Finally he said, "You want to talk some football, Charlie?"

"I always want to talk football."

That is what they did, the old man even pulling a piece of paper and a pen out of his back pocket, taking a few notes to himself as they went position by position, going through the strengths and weaknesses of the Bulldogs.

At one point Joe Warren said, "You won't ever lie to me, will you, Charlie? Or just tell me what you think I want to hear?"

"No, sir."

"Good."

But he looked more than tired in that moment, he looked sad, Charlie wanting in the worst way to take the sad look off his face in the middle of what felt like such a great day. He wanted to do something *right now* to justify the old man's confidence in him, his trust, his friendship.

"I never talk much about my dad, Mr. Warren," Charlie said, "not with anybody except my mom, and even her not so much. He left when I was little and never came back and I don't think he's ever going to come back. He doesn't ever talk to my mom and he doesn't ever talk to me."

"Anna told me about him," the old man said. "Or as much as she knows about him."

"I'm not telling you that because I want you to feel sorry for me, Mr. Warren," Charlie said. "I'm telling you because I just think that no matter how bad things might seem sometimes between you and Matt, well, it just seems to me those aren't such bad problems to have."

Joe Warren smiled then, smiled like he meant it, reached over and squeezed Charlie's hand.

"Charlie, my boy, I'm awfully glad of something."

"What's that?" Charlie said.

"You're not just my football friend," he said. "You're my friend, period."

They went back to talking football after that until Anna came out of the trees looking for them, saying that her mom was here and it was time to go.

The next day thirty-eight-year-old Tom Pinkett threw three touchdown passes and no interceptions as Charlie watched with Anna and her grandfather from his suite.

And the Bulldogs went to 1–0, upsetting the 49ers.

Ten

TWO THINGS HAPPENED THE NEXT week, both huge in Charlie's universe.

First: Finding out that Kevin Fallon's dad was going to play Charlie's fantasy picks from *The Charlie Show* on *his* nightly radio show. Kevin and his dad had listened to the podcast and Mr. Fallon thought his listeners would get a kick out of a twelve-year-old being this informed about pro football, especially a kid from his own Pop Warner team. So he said that if Charlie was willing they'd give it a shot, see how the audience reacted, think about making it a regular segment.

Charlie "Brain" Gaines on E-S-P-N radio.

Second huge deal: Joe Warren invited Charlie to watch practice with him on Thursday, telling him that he'd asked Anna to come along, too, but was reminded she had a piano lesson that couldn't be moved. It was her mother's idea, Anna learning a musical instrument, a fact that Anna was constantly reminding Charlie of, telling him her mother thought music would make her more of a lady.

She always put air quotes around "lady."

"I'm wondering," Anna said to him one time, "if Mom wants me to be the kind of musical lady that somebody like Lady Gaga is. Or that other famous lady, Miley Cyrus."

But of course she had gotten really good at piano really fast, despite her constant grumbling that it was taking her away from sports, and Charlie knew she actually looked forward to her lessons. Just not tomorrow, because she would rather have been at Bulldogs practice with Charlie and her gramps.

On Wednesday night, Charlie and Anna were at her house, up in her room, waiting for the last fifteen minutes of Mr. Fallon's show . . . and for Charlie's debut on ESPN radio.

They'd finished the second *Charlie Show* that afternoon over at Charlie's house, then gone to Anna's for dinner, Charlie's mom having another late night at the studio.

Now they waited through the calls and guests on Mr. Fallon's show. To Charlie the show usually felt like one more place on the dial you could go to for nonstop Bulldogs bashing. Yet not this week, not after the way Tom Pinkett and the whole team had played in the opener. Even Steve Fallon—normally one of the bashing kings of L.A. radio—was being nice tonight, though what he was mostly doing was telling listeners to enjoy the team's victory while they could, before this week's princes turned into next week's frogs.

"These are the two hours of the day when I don't like Kevin's dad very much," Anna said. "He's mean even when he's trying to sound nice."

"I don't think he means it," Charlie said. "Most guys on the radio, and you know how much I listen to the radio, say stuff just to draw attention to themselves. And usually think they're funnier than they actually are."

"Mean is still mean."

"How about all the mean things *you* say about your own family's team?"

"To you," she said. "I say them to you. You never hear me do it in front of other kids. Not even Kevin."

"But you do mean *your* mean things."

Anna laughed. "Soooooo much."

Steve Fallon had been taking calls for most of the last half hour, Charlie thinking the comments were mostly boneheaded, people acting as if they had no idea what they were watching when they watched the Bulldogs play. Mr. Fallon had begun the last hour of his show, which ran from seven to nine, interviewing one of the radio broadcasters from the Ravens, who Charlie thought sounded like just another caller, only with a deeper voice.

Like he should have just identified himself as Bob from Baltimore.

Finally—*finally*—with about eight minutes left in the show, Mr. Fallon introduced the clip with Charlie, explaining that he played on a team with his son, Kevin, that he was known as Brain to his teammates, and was practically like the pinball wizard of fantasy football.

"What's a pinball wizard?" Charlie said.

"No clue," Anna said.

"By the way?" he said. "I pretty much could have gone the rest of my life without being called 'Brain' on the radio."

"Deal," she said. Her way of telling him to deal with it.

Then she was shushing him, even though she was the last one talking, because there was Charlie's voice coming out of her radio, from the clip Mr. Fallon was using from *The Charlie Show*.

He listened to himself make his picks, talking about the points he'd picked up in Week One, talking about a trade he'd made already, talking about how his kicker—from the Texans—had made three long field goals in Houston's opener, getting him even more points from that position than he'd expected. Who to sit and who to watch and how his team defense, the Giants, had not only shut out the Eagles, but scored two defensive touchdowns and had six sacks.

Charlie tried to act like it was no big deal, tried not to act excited in front of Anna.

Knowing he was ridiculously excited.

"You sounded like a pro," Anna said when she shut off the radio.

"I sounded like a small dog. I'm just glad I didn't have to do it live."

"You could have." Anna smiled. "Dog."

"Mr. Fallon said maybe down the road. For now if he just takes some of our show, he can play it whenever he wants in his show and I don't have to sit around waiting for him to call me."

"You know I'd be all over you if it wasn't any good," she said.

"Tell me about it."

"But it *was* good. Really good. Really."

"I wonder if anybody was really listening."

"Just wait, Charlie Gaines," she said. "Just wait for the reaction from people who really were listening, and are about to find out how much of a Brain you really are about football."

He didn't mind when she said it.

"If I'm so brilliant, how come you disagree with me so often?"

She smiled right at him. Charlie wondering, and not for the first time when he was with her, how old you had to be to tell a girl how much you loved a smile like hers; if you had to wait until you were in high school.

"Being a brain doesn't mean always being right," she said. Still smiling she added, "Deal with that, too."

Eleven

MR. WARREN'S DRIVER, CARLOS, PICKED up Charlie at eleven sharp the next morning for the ride to practice. Charlie didn't know a lot about cars or have much interest in them, even living in Los Angeles, but he knew enough to recognize that he was riding in the backseat of a shiny black Mercedes.

Something else he didn't know:

Whether he was supposed to talk to the driver or not.

But then it was Carlos who started talking about the Bulldogs, Charlie figuring out quickly that he knew his football, and loved his L.A. Bulldogs almost as much as he loved Joe Warren.

"He deserves so much better," Carlos said. He had volunteered to Charlie that he had been born in Mexico, but had hardly any accent.

Charlie said, "Maybe last week is the start of something, and they're going to surprise us this season."

Looked up from the backseat, saw Carlos looking at him in the rearview mirror. Grinning.

"*De tus labios a los oídos de Dios,*" he said.

"I'm bad at Spanish."

Carlos said, "From your lips to God's ears, young man."

When they got to Bulldogs Stadium they used the players' entrance for cars, went down a long ramp, Charlie starting to think that the next stop for them might be the fifty-yard line. Eventually they parked in a space that Carlos said was only about fifty yards from the Bulldogs' locker room. The sign on the wall in front of them said "Mr. Warren, Sr."

Next to them was a fancy red convertible, top down. The sign in front of that one said "Mr. Warren, Jr."

And on the other side of that, Carlos told him, was the Jeep Laredo belonging to the team's head coach, Nick Fiore.

Charlie and Anna had talked about Coach Fiore, whom they both liked. Everyone in the media seemed to agree that Nick Fiore's job was on the line this season. For once, even Charlie and Anna agreed that it wasn't fair to blame Coach Fiore, that you could only coach the players you had. Anna always adding, "The players my uncle drafted or traded for."

But even at the age of twelve, Charlie had figured out that nobody had ever passed a law saying sports had to be fair.

Any more than life had to be.

Carlos and Charlie rode up to Mr. Warren's office in a private elevator, the office one level below his suite, a whole wall of windows behind his desk looking down at the field.

There were two men standing at the windows with their backs to the office, watching practice.

"Mr. Warren," Carlos said, "your guest is here."

Joe Warren's sweater was a light blue today, but other than that he looked the same as he had at the house the day before the opener. The younger guy standing next to him, Charlie knew right away, was Matt Warren, the Bulldogs' general manager.

Mr. Warren's son. Anna's uncle.

And the guy most local sports fans, at least the loudest ones, thought was responsible for the team being as bad as it had been since its first season, whether they'd just won the first game of this season or not.

"Charlie," Matt Warren said, coming around his dad's desk to shake Charlie's hand. "Good to see you."

They'd met briefly in Mr. Warren's suite during the Panthers preseason game, Matt just stopping in for a few minutes.

"Nice to see you again, Mr. Warren."

"Call me Matt. My dad's the Mr. Warren in the family."

"See how they treat you when you're as old as Sunset Boulevard?" Joe Warren said.

His son said, "We're just standing here wondering if the team we're looking at can get to 2–0 against the Ravens."

"We've never done that," Charlie said. "Started 2–0."

Matt Warren raised his eyebrows and said, "You weren't joking about this kid. He knows his stuff."

"I do believe I might have mentioned that in passing," Joe Warren said, winking at Charlie.

"Tell me about it," Matt said. "Charlie, my dad spends more time these days talking football with you than he actually does talking football with me."

"I guess I'm as lucky as you are," Charlie said. "Getting to talk football with him, I mean."

"Young people make old people feel less old," Joe Warren said. "Sometimes the younger the better."

Joe Warren motioned Charlie to come around the desk and stand with them at the windows. There were players and coaches all over the field, the players in full pads, offense scrimmaging against the defense, Matt Warren explaining to Charlie how they'd changed the rules in the last few years, the NFL reducing the number of full-contact practices. A lot of it had to do with the attention brought to concussions and brain injuries, but the players' association had bargained for it, Matt Warren said, thinking it might lengthen careers.

All of which Charlie knew, but he wasn't going to tell Matt Warren that.

On the field Tom Pinkett threw a bullet pass over the middle, then floated a deep ball just over the hands of defensive back Ray Milner—Charlie knew who it was before he saw the number—and into the hands of the best wide receiver out of all the ones Matt Warren had drafted, Harrison Mays.

"I have to admit," Matt Warren said, "I never thought the old guy would throw like he did last Sunday ever again, at least not in a real game." Shook his head and said, "Most yards he's thrown for in ten years."

This time, Charlie couldn't help himself, didn't hold back what he already knew.

"Actually," he said to Matt Warren, "he had that one game

three years ago when he came off the bench for the Titans and went crazy and ended up throwing for more than that."

Matt Warren turned and smiled at Charlie. The kind of smile you got from your parents—or your parent—when they were trying to be patient with you without coming out and telling you that you'd just said something that was dumber than hamsters.

"Not for three-fifty," Matt said.

"Three ninety-two," Charlie said.

He was a guest here, even if he wasn't Matt Warren's guest. But this was football. And in football the numbers mattered. Maybe more to Charlie Gaines than to anybody.

So even though he knew he should have dropped it, he hadn't. He turned and saw Joe Warren smiling at his son the same way Matt Warren had just smiled at Charlie, Charlie thinking the old man's eyes were full of mischief as he said to his son, "Why don't you check on that fancy phone of yours."

"Really, Dad?"

"Just for the fun of it."

Matt Warren sighed, knowing he had no choice in the matter, not in front of Charlie. He pulled his iPhone out of his back pocket, moving his thumbs across the keys on the screen like he was sending a fast text.

Then he put the phone away and shrugged. "Turns out you were right, Charlie. Titans against the Colts. In Indy. Twenty-four out of thirty-eight, for three hundred ninety-two yards. Three TDs and a pick. Guy bounced around so much, I lost track of him."

"Well," Charlie said, not wanting this whole scene to get any more awkward than it already was, "we were both sort of right. Tom hadn't thrown that way in a while."

"Charlie boy's a fantasy whiz, I probably mentioned that, too," Joe Warren said. "In passing."

On the field, they'd moved the offense back to its own twenty-yard line and Tom Pinkett threw another long ball, this one to Maurice James, another one of the Bulldogs' high-draft-choice wideouts from two years ago. He was the biggest talker on the team, constantly complaining that nobody would toss him the rock, as he put it, at least not often enough to keep him happy.

But Matt Warren barely seemed to notice, turning to his father and saying, "You've been talking about Charlie and fantasy football so much lately I think I need to get you into a league."

"Me? With a team in a fantasy league?" Joe Warren said with a wink. "Well, that's just the craziest thing I've ever heard. I'm busy enough just owning one team."

Charlie grinned, knowing Joe Warren was playing a bit of a game with the two of them.

"Speaking of our beloved Bulldogs, isn't there something you'd like to say to Charlie boy, Matt?"

Matt Warren sighed and Charlie thought his face started to redden. Yet his voice sounded sincere. "I had my doubts. Yet if Tom Pinkett keeps playing the way he did against the 49ers, he really could be more than a *one*-game changer. So if I haven't officially thanked you, I'm doing that now."

Charlie, smiling back, said, "You're welcome."

Matt said, "I know everybody, starting with my dad, is stuck on the subject of Tom Pinkett right now. But I think we've all got to take a deep breath and remember he can't be a one-man team."

"I'm not stuck on him," Joe Warren said. "Unless the definition of stuck means being pleasantly surprised."

"What else have we been talking about for the past week," Matt said. "How you think the Dodgers are going to do down the stretch against the Giants?"

Still smiling, even though Charlie didn't think he meant it all that much at the moment.

"Anyway," Matt said, "one of my jobs around here right now is to keep reminding everybody it really did count for just one win from Charlie's quarterback. And I need to keep thinking of other ways to improve our team."

"For which your father is constantly grateful, if I haven't mentioned that to you lately."

Matt started to say something, kept it inside instead. Then he told Charlie he'd see him around, told his dad he'd talk to him later, turned and left, Charlie feeling in that moment as if a whole lot of tension had left the room with him.

"Sometimes he thinks I'm putting more pressure on him than I really am," Joe Warren said finally. "It's not as easy as it looks to run a team."

He sat down now, pulled back the middle drawer of his desk, took out a small pill bottle, popped one into his mouth, drank it down with water. Saw Charlie watching him.

"Don't worry," Joe Warren said. "Pill taking is as much a part of being old as forgetting where you put your reading glasses." He smiled. Small one. "Or getting stuck on things and annoying your children."

He slapped his palms on the desk, stood up, said to Charlie, "Okay: Do we watch practice from up here, or down on the field?"

"No-brainer," the boy known as Brain said. "Field."

"Thought so," Joe Warren said. "Let's go down there and remind ourselves that football is still supposed to be fun." He smiled again. "For football fans old and young."

They took the elevator down and walked through a tunnel and then up a runway and then everything in front of Charlie was green grass and blue sky.

He was on the practice field with his team.

Not Joe Warren's team in that moment.

His.

As soon as one of the equipment managers saw Joe Warren on the field, Charlie saw him running toward another runway, one closer to the Bulldogs' locker room. What felt like a minute later, he came riding out on the field with a golf cart that had a roof on it, drove it right over to where the old man and Charlie were standing, at the end of the home team's bench.

The old man said to Charlie, "They need to bring me my own shade."

The two of them sat down in the cart and Joe Warren took the wheel, promising Charlie he'd let him have a turn later. Charlie said that he was totally down with that.

Then they watched as Tom Pinkett and the offense kept scrimmaging right in front of them, like football was finally close
enough for Charlie to wrap his arms around it, Charlie hearing
the grunts and the thud of contact, not to mention some of the
most colorful and creative swearing he'd ever heard in his life.

"When you get home later and your mother asks how your day
went," Joe Warren said, "please leave out the part about the salty
language."

"My mom says you can never shock her with bad words. Part
of her job requires saying no to agents."

The old man laughed. *A good sound*, Charlie thought.

Practice went on. Neither one of them spoke, Charlie concen-
trating, trying to take in everything at once. *Observating*, Anna
would call it. At one point Charlie took a couple of pictures with
his phone, just to have something to show Kevin Fallon tomorrow
at his own practice.

They had been there about half an hour when Joe Warren said,
"Let's play a little game."

"Don't make it a hard one," Charlie said. "I'm having too good
a time."

"As am I, Charlie boy. As am I."

"I don't know why this feels even way cooler than getting to
come to games, but it does," Charlie said.

"Maybe it's because the stands are empty," the old man said.
"It feels like the sport belongs just to us."

Nailed it on the head, Charlie thought.

"So what's the game, Mr. Warren?"

"A game of pretend," he said. "Think of it as a different kind of fantasy football."

"Okaaaaay."

"Every football fan's fantasy is to own their own team, right? Let's pretend for the next little while that the Bulldogs are really yours, and not mine."

Wait for it, as Anna liked to say.

"Tell me what you'd do if it was your team to make it better."

"You mean it?"

"Hardly ever say anything I don't, son," Joe Warren said. "Thought you knew that already."

Charlie took in some air. Then he swallowed. Just buying himself a little bit of time.

Then he said, "We're as good as a lot of contenders on both lines, especially on defense. But if we don't improve our linebackers and secondary, we're never going to beat anybody."

He kept going from there.

Charlie Gaines talking football with someone listening to every word he said. Yeah. A *whole* different kind of fantasy football.

Twelve

AFTER HIS OWN PRACTICE THAT night with the Cardinals, Charlie told Kevin Fallon some of what had happened with Mr. Warren, but not all of it, saving the best parts for when he met up with Anna later at Cold Stone.

Kevin and him lying in the grass a little after six o'clock, away from the other guys, Charlie waiting for his mom to pick him up.

"You know," Kevin said, "if it were me that had gone to practice with the owner of the team . . ."

"Which it wasn't," Charlie said.

"But if it *were* me," Kevin continued, "I'd already have the pictures up on Facebook, and right now I'd be telling the whole team."

"But I'm not you," Charlie said.

They were good friends, as different as they were. Starting with what different players they were, how good Kevin was at football, and how Charlie would have given anything to be that good. To *be* Kevin out on that field. Be that kind of star running back.

Off the field, though, Kevin struggled sometimes—or Charlie struggled *with* having him as a friend—mostly because Kevin thought everything that had ever happened to him in his life was the most interesting thing that had ever happened to anybody.

And couldn't wait to broadcast it. Like he was the real broadcaster in his family and not his dad.

Charlie was used to it by now, and tried not to let it bother him too much, just because he knew there was so much more good than bad to Kevin Fallon, the two not even close if he was listing all the good things. Big mouth, but a big heart, too. Charlie knew how generous Kevin was, and how every year at Father's Night at school Kevin would have his dad pick Charlie up so they could all go together. Wouldn't ever let Charlie skip the event. He knew how hard Kevin had worked in the summer trying to get Charlie to be a better football player, working with him on his agility, showing him how to be better in pass coverage, telling him all the time, "If you can even come close to staying with me, you can stay with anybody, dude."

Still: There was no way on earth that Charlie was telling Kevin about things getting a little tense between Mr. Warren and Matt Warren in that office. Or Mr. Warren quizzing Charlie about the Bulldogs' roster when they were on the field in the golf cart, Mr. Warren treating Charlie like he was his new scouting director.

On the field now with Kevin, Charlie said, "This stays between us, right? Like, *really* between us?"

Charlie had pulled his cell phone out of his gym bag because he'd promised Kevin he'd show him a few of the pictures he'd taken. "I don't want Mr. Warren thinking that I've got a big mouth."

It got a grin out of Kevin. "You mean like mine."

"You said it, not me. But we've got a deal, right?"

"Yes. Now show me the pictures before I have to beat you."

Charlie did. Kevin not believing how close Charlie had been to the action, even if it was practice and not a game. Kevin scrolled through the pictures and then did it again, commenting on every one, like he was giving some sort of slide-show presentation. Then Charlie told him about what a cool guy Carlos was, the guy who'd driven him to practice. How he'd met Coach Fiore, even congratulated him on the team's big win over the 49ers, and how Coach had said:

"I'll tell you what I told the team before practice today, Charlie. If we don't make it happen again next week, it will be as if last week didn't happen. And people will think we're the same old Dogs."

"You get to talk to any of the players?" Kevin asked.

"I wish."

"Who would you most want to talk to?"

Charlie didn't even have to think about it. "Tom Pinkett." There was no way he was telling Kevin why, though.

"Yeah, well, good luck with that one," Kevin said. "Even my dad has never gotten a one-on-one with Tom Pinkett no matter how hard he's tried."

"Can't tell your dad about any of this."

"Our deal applies to my father?"

"Especially to your father."

Kevin's mom called to him from behind the bench, telling him it was time to go. Kevin asked Charlie if he needed a ride and Charlie said, no, he was good, his mom would be here any minute.

"Some day for you," Kevin said.

"You have no idea," Charlie said.

Knowing he had left out plenty, not just about the scene between father and son before he went down to the field, and not just about all the talking about the team he'd done with Mr. Warren in that golf cart.

Joe Warren had also told Charlie before he left that he could come to practice at least once a week.

More than that, if he could manage with his football and school schedule.

"Think of it as your new after-school job," the old man had said.

Then he'd winked at Charlie again, like that was a way for the two of them to seal the deal.

Thirteen

"GRAMPS SAID THAT?" ANNA SAID. "For real? He called it an after-school *job*?"

They had gotten their ice cream at Cold Stone, brought it with them to their favorite bench in Media Park, not so far from Sony Studios.

"He said he wants me to be his other set of eyes," Charlie said, "as often as I can."

"That is *so* crisp," Anna said.

One of her favorite expressions. The progression, as far as Charlie could tell, was cool to fresh to crisp.

Crisp was as good as it got.

She ate more ice cream out of a big cup. Chocolate Devotion was her favorite flavor, smothered in chocolate sauce and chocolate sprinkles. Charlie knew that if Anna were forced to choose between chocolate and football, she would have to give some serious thought to that.

"It's weird," Charlie said. "Your grandfather has really only known me for a week, and he acts as if he's known me as long as he's known you."

"You're kind of easy to get to know," she said

"He's a very cool guy, your Gramps," Charlie said. "I can see it when he's with you."

"He'd like it more if I were a boy," she said. "He's still hoping that when Matt gets married, his wife has a boy."

"He's not going to love any grandson more than he loves you," Charlie said. "Trust me on that one."

"Really?" she said. "Old guys like Gramps still think that sports is more of a guy thing. Like, he'd never ever think of me running the Bulldogs when I grow up."

"Women have owned teams," Charlie said.

"Yeah," Anna said, "when their husband who owned the team before them up and died."

He'd never heard her talk about this stuff before, not like this. She turned to face him now. She had finished her ice cream and the last of Charlie's and had her legs crossed underneath her and a Bulldogs cap on her head, hair spilling out of the opening in the back.

"Oh, Gramps knows how much I love football and how much I know about football. But he can't help himself, he still sees me as his little baby girl."

"Well, technically, aren't you a little girl to him?"

"This isn't a debate, Gaines."

Putting some snap into her voice.

"Got it."

She shook her head. "He looks at me and still sees the four-year-old who used to sit on his lap while he explained everything that was happening in the game."

"Amazing!" Charlie said. "That's exactly the way I see you, except I don't want you to sit in my lap!"

"When I'm being serious you'd better be serious, mister. Or we're going to have a problem. Even after ice cream."

"I wasn't *not* being serious," he said. "I was just trying to be funny for a second. And that was funny right there."

"Was it?"

"Little bit?" Charlie said.

"Whatever," she said.

"I'll take that as a yes," he said.

"Can we get back to what we were talking about before your *attempt* at humor?"

"Proceed."

"Anyway, I'm just saying that it's not surprising that Gramps would rather hang with you at practice than with me."

"So . . . are we good, you and me?" Charlie suddenly feeling as uncomfortable as he did earlier with Matt Warren.

"Good as Cold Stone," Anna said, yet still with an edge to her voice.

Charlie had a feeling he'd be smart to change the subject.

"It was weird being in the middle of your grandfather and uncle like that."

"That's sounds like the most amazing part of the whole day," she said. "That Uncle Matt couldn't even stop himself from acting stressed in front of you."

"It got a little awkward there."

"Sounds like. I've seen it happen with them before."

"It wasn't that bad, I just sort of wanted to not be there."

"Uncle Matt probably didn't want to be there, with *you*, either. He's been wrong about so many players and now you turn out to be right about his new quarterback."

"I felt bad for him," Charlie said. "I mean, put yourself in his position. If this were happening to you, you'd feel a little defensive, wouldn't you?"

"No doubt," she said. "I'll give you that. But you've got to admit something: As bad as you say you felt, you felt really *good* being right about Tom Pinkett."

"Not at that moment, I didn't."

"You admit right now you at least liked it a little," she said, poking him with a finger to his chest.

He smiled. "Okay, maybe a tiny bit."

"Ha! I knew I was right."

"Happy now?"

"I'm always happy when I'm right," she said.

"No wonder you're so happy all the time."

"Exactly," she said.

They sat and watched people walk their dogs. And toss footballs. And Frisbees. It was what Charlie always thought of as a magical time of the day in Southern California, when a special light came over the place and it wasn't day anymore yet not quite night.

"You know what probably made Uncle Matt even madder?" she said. "Seeing Gramps with you in that golf cart later, the two of you chatting away."

"Why would he care about that?"

"Because *he* wants to be the only extra set of eyes that Gramps needs. That's why."

Fourteen

THE CULVER CITY CARDINALS' NEXT game was against the Redondo Beach Lions, at Redondo Beach's field, the day before the Bulldogs would play the Ravens in Baltimore.

When Coach Dayley gathered the players around him before the kickoff, he told them what he knew about the Lions. He'd talked to his friend who coached Palos Verdes—the Palos Verdes Vikings had faced Redondo Beach in their opener—and found out the Lions were big and physical and loved running the ball so much they might not throw ten passes the whole game.

"Might be one of those low-scoring deals today," Coach Dayley said. "But I'm good with that, long as we're the ones who did the most scoring at the end."

Not only was it a low-scoring game into the third quarter, it was a no-scoring game. Both teams had had one good chance in the first half. But Jarrod Benedict had fumbled on Redondo Beach's five-yard line when he'd try to keep it himself and score on an option play.

When it looked as if the Lions might take the lead right before halftime, having driven the ball from their own twenty, about half the Cardinals' defense—Charlie included, in there for a big moment—stuffed their fullback on a fourth-and-goal from the two.

So it stayed 0–0 into the third quarter. It had started to rain by then, Charlie not even able to remember the last time he'd played football in the rain. Sometimes he couldn't even remember playing football when it was cloudy. The rain didn't affect the Vikings too much, since they didn't want to throw anyway. But mostly the Cardinals' offense had become Jarrod either pitching it to Kevin Fallon or keeping it himself, Coach Dayley constantly reminding them to hold on to the ball. If anything was going to decide this game—provided anybody scored—it was probably going to be a turnover.

Charlie had spent most of the third quarter standing next to Coach Dayley, studying the Redondo Beach quarterback, wondering why his coach didn't let him throw the ball more. The guy seemed to have a good arm, even with a slippery ball.

But as it rained harder, the Lions' coach seemed to shut down his passing game completely. Like he thought the same thing that Coach Dayley did, that the game might be decided by a turnover, and putting a slick ball in the air only increased the risk.

So neither team had moved the ball past midfield as the game slogged through the mud to the fourth quarter, both punters probably getting more play than they would all season, both quarterbacks always seeming to start deep in their own territory. On the sideline, Charlie didn't just feel as if he were watching a game played in the mud, he felt as if both offenses were playing the game uphill.

It was the Lions who finally got the ball past midfield, into Cardinals' territory, barely, first down at the Cardinals' forty-nine, with two minutes to go. It was then that Shota Matsumoto, one of the Cardinals' best players at outside linebacker, twisted his ankle trying to cut in the mud.

Shota didn't even wait for help, just pointed to himself as he hobbled off the field. As he did, Coach Dayley said, "Get in there, Charlie."

Second game of the season, tie game, fourth quarter, the guy they called Brain in there trying to do what the starters on defense were trying to do in the mud:

Get the ball back, get the game.

The Lions' quarterback kept it twice on runs, got four yards the first time, five yards the second. It was third-and-one for the Lions at the Cardinals' forty-yard line. Charlie took his place as right outside linebacker, saw the Lions come out of the huddle.

And put his hands in the air to call the Cardinals' second-to-last time-out. Just like he'd done in practice that day, after asking Coach Fallon if it was all right.

Dropping down and untying his shoelaces and retying them, like that was the reason he needed to stop play.

Charlie gave a quick look over at the Cardinals' sideline, saw Coach Dayley with his hands on his hips, head cocked to the side. Glaring at him. His look saying: What just happened here?

Sean Barkley, their fastest and best defensive back, playing safety today, loudest kid on the team, came running up to Charlie.

"Brain," he said, "you lost that mind of yours Coach is always talkin up? Like, you think we're not gonna need that time-out later to win this game?"

Charlie kept his head down.

"Sean," Charlie said, "you gotta trust me: They're gonna throw deep. They're going for the win on this play."

"Okay, now you did up and lose your mind. You see that they don't even have a whole yard to make another first down? You do see that, right?"

"Sean, you were at corner the one time they threw deep. But it's the only time they've had two guys lined up behind the quarterback. The other times they've been back there, they split them. He's gonna go play-action again to the tight end. He thinks we *won't* think he'll do that. But he's gonna go for it all."

"You're really down with the coach-on-the-field stuff, aren't you?" Sean said.

Charlie stood up. "I'm gonna blitz," he said. "You stay with the tight end. That ball goes up, it's gonna be yours."

"You know the deal on this, right?" Sean said. "You better be right."

"I sort of know that."

Charlie thinking: I've *got* to be right, or I won't make it off special teams the rest of the season.

The refs started the play clock. The Lions' quarterback—Charlie was pretty sure he'd heard one of his teammates call him Nick in the first half—took the snap from under center, turned, and looked like he was executing a perfect reverse-pivot handoff to his fullback.

Charlie flying—well, as close as he came to flying—from the outside as Nick pulled the ball back.

He'd been right.

A play-action fake all the way.

Charlie coming hard as he could from the outside, trying not to slip down.

Trusting that Sean was somewhere behind him, running step-for-step with the Lions' tight end.

Charlie wasn't fast enough, even unblocked, to get to the quarterback, certainly not on a wet field. But what he could do was let out a yell, trying to sound as fierce as he felt in that moment, letting the kid know he was coming, getting him to give a quick turn of his head before he looked down the field and let the ball go.

It was enough, just barely enough, for the QB to rush his throw. Then Charlie went plowing into him, a legal hit, and they both went into the mud, Charlie getting a faceful of it before he rolled over, scrambled to his feet, and tried to see what was happening down the field.

Which was this:

Sean Barkley with the ball, cutting toward the sideline, being chased by a lot of dirty Redondo Beach uniforms that had looked very brand-spanking-new and very white at the start of the game. Sean had made the interception that gave the Cardinals the chance they needed.

Charlie tried to throw a block on one of their O-linemen,

missed. The Lions' quarterback, up on his feet now, managed to knock Sean out of bounds, but not until he had reached the Redondo Beach thirteen-yard line.

Cardinals' ball, a minute and ten seconds to go. Sean Barkley and Charlie jogged all the way across the field together, Sean giving Charlie the first high five he'd ever given him.

"Brain and the blitz," Sean Barkley said. "Love it."

Charlie just kept his head down, kept running, Coach Dayley coming out to meet him, ten yards at least from the white line.

"Just tell me what you saw," he said.

Charlie told him.

Coach was staring at Charlie in a different way now.

"They used that formation just the one time?"

Charlie nodded.

Coach shook his head, handed Charlie his clipboard, the pages on it soaking wet. All Charlie could see were ink stains running in all directions.

Coach Dayley said, "You need this more than I do."

And Charlie said, "Just doing my job."

"Calling a one-man blitz for yourself after you call your own time-out?"

Charlie shrugged, grinned, and said, "Part of the job of being a player-coach, Coach."

With all the momentum and positive energy on their side now, it took the Cardinals just three plays from there, Kevin Fallon doing all of the heavy lifting, being the star he was supposed to be.

The last carry was something to see, Kevin breaking a play

that was supposed to take him up the middle off-tackle, getting to the sideline, and launching himself off the mud and over the goal line—like this sleek but very dirty bird—with the touchdown that made the final score 6–0 for the Cardinals.

Charlie found out at lunch on Monday that *The Charlie Show* had turned him into an instant celebrity at Culver City Middle, in a way that even being the king of his fantasy leagues never had.

"Did you get an agent yet?" Lizzie Hartong said when she came over to sit down with Charlie and Anna and Kevin.

"Yeah," Charlie said. "Next there's probably going to be a billboard of me on Sunset Boulevard, all because of one podcast."

"The billboard could be a problem," Anna said.

"Why's that?" Kevin said.

"How am I gonna climb up there and draw a mustache on Charlie's face?" Anna said.

Lizzie said, "Oooh, can I black out his teeth?"

"Great," Charlie said. "Suddenly I'm sitting at the mean-girl table."

Anna and Lizzie high-fived each other. "And loving it," Anna said.

When Lizzie went to put her tray back in the rack, Charlie said, "When did you and Lizzie become such funny friends?"

Anna said, "When it was time to make fun of you, of course."

After that a bunch of guys came over to the table, telling Charlie they thought it was about ten stages of awesome that he was actually on a real L.A. sports talk show.

Brad Bates said Charlie was on his way to becoming an Internet sensation.

"I just got lucky with some picks, is all," Charlie said.

"Lucky?" Brad said. "Dude, you've been crushing it ever since you told people to jump on Tom Pinkett."

The Bulldogs were 1–1, having lost their second game to the Ravens in Baltimore on a late field goal. But Tom *had* played well again, had thrown three more touchdown passes, and seemed to be taking the Bulldogs down the field for another upset win when a perfect pass went right through tight end Mo Bettencourt's hands—usually the surest hands on the team—and got intercepted, setting up the Ravens' winning kick with twenty-two seconds left.

The Bulldogs that close to being 2–0 for the first time in their history.

Still: Last year they hadn't won their first game until Week Five. They had played well in Baltimore against a playoff team, done it on the road. Charlie knew that a loss was a loss. But also knew enough about sports to know that there were actually good losses sometimes.

This was going to be a good day to talk about the Bulldogs on the latest installment of *The Charlie Show*. Anna also told him to remind the listeners about all the good picks he'd made the week before.

"I feel funny doing that," he said when they were setting up in his room.

"That's the whole point of being in the media, dummy, drawing as much attention to yourself as possible. It's practically a law they passed. Besides, the more you're right with your picks, the more people are going to talk up *The Charlie Show* even if some of that talk is just lips flapping. After you left the table today, Kevin said that he could be the one to do a show like this, that he knows almost as much about football as you do. But I set him straight on that one, don't worry."

"You're the boss."

"Finally you understand that."

"It's what my mom calls the path of least resistance." Adding: "Boss."

"Oh, now you're being sarcastic?" Anna said. "Because if you are, I will go home and you can try this yourself."

"Yes, *sir!*" he said, but with a smile, so she'd know he was kidding.

"You keep going like this and the next stop is going to be *Jimmy Kimmel.*"

"How can I be on a show that I can't stay up late enough to watch?"

She gave him a soft punch on the shoulder. "You'll just need to grow up a little."

They did the podcast then. Anna talked even more than usual this week, asking more questions, mostly about last week's picks, making sure herself that the listeners were reminded about how well he'd done.

That night, Charlie's picks were back on Mr. Fallon's show.

It was right at the end of the show that Kevin's dad said that not only was Charlie Gaines this kind of rock star at fantasy football, he was just as good at spotting talent in real football.

Meaning Bulldogs football.

It was then that Charlie heard what everybody listening to the show heard, Mr. Fallon saying that it was twelve-year-old Charlie Gaines who told Joe Warren to sign Tom Pinkett, over the objections of his son, Matt.

Fifteen

CHARLIE CALLED HER BEFORE SHE called him. Didn't even say hello.

"How did he find out?" Charlie said. "Tell me you didn't tell Kevin."

She didn't say anything at first.

Then: "I did. But I can explain."

"You told Kevin," Charlie said. "And he told his dad. Perfect."

He reached over and shut off the radio, just as some other announcer was giving out baseball scores at the top of the hour.

"I'm so sorry," Anna said, and sounded like she was, but Charlie didn't care in that moment.

"You told *Kevin*?" he said. "Why didn't you just put it out over the Internet? You're the one who's always saying it's a good thing his heart is bigger than his big mouth."

"Can I at least explain?"

"Before you do, let me ask you something," Charlie said. "How big a deal is this going to be? Are people really going to care about a dumb story like this?"

Knowing her answer before he asked the question.

"It's gonna be a big deal, not gonna lie," she answered. "It's L.A., it's the Bulldogs, it's football."

"Now it's me."

"And now it's you."

He was still trying to process what he'd just heard, hearing himself treated like he'd turned into the sports news of the day, and how it was his best friend in the world who'd helped put it out there.

Anna said, "Remember me telling you that Kevin was giving me some chirp about how he should have been the one to get on his dad's show? That would have been annoying enough, but then he started acting as if he knew as much about football as you." She paused before adding, "As much as you and as much as me."

"The other day, you mean. I remember."

"Do you remember me saying how I set him straight?"

Charlie said he kind of remembered. It didn't seem like that huge a deal at the time.

He could hear her blow out some air at her end of the phone.

"Well, that's how I set him straight," she said. "I told him not to tell anybody, but if he knew so much about football, how come it was you and not him who told Gramps to sign Tom Pinkett?"

She said Kevin then accused her of making it up, saying his dad had told him it had to have been her uncle Matt who came up with the idea, even if Matt Warren had been in the papers saying it was an "organizational" decision. Acting as if somehow he and his dad knew as much about the whole thing as Anna did.

That, she said, just chafed her even more, so she told Kevin even stronger than before that it had been Charlie, not her uncle, that Kevin didn't know what he was talking about and neither did his dad.

"So you treated it like another competition," Charlie said. "You wanted to make sure he knew that *you* knew more stuff than he did. Awesome, Anna. Truly. Awesome."

He was on his bed, head back on his pillows, eyes closed. Charlie pretending that as soon as he opened them, the whole thing would be like a dream—or a nightmare—ending as soon as he woke up from it.

He wasn't so worried about his secret, if you could even call it a secret, being out there now as much as he was worried that he had put Mr. Warren in a bad spot.

"I feel bad enough about this," Anna said. "Don't try to make me feel worse."

"Oh," Charlie said. "I'm the one who's supposed to be sorry."

"He was just annoying me *so* much. I told him that all of our guys thought Pinkett was washed-up at first. And Kevin said, 'So your grandfather listened to Charlie instead of his own son? A twelve-year-old instead of the team GM?' I said, 'Yeah, genius, that was pretty much the deal.' But I made him swear that he wouldn't tell anybody, and he said he was cool with that."

"You should have told me what you meant by 'handling it,'" Charlie said. "I would have talked to Kevin myself and told him that he couldn't tell, that it would be a total suckfest if the news got out."

"He should have been able to figure that out himself," Anna said. "He's not an idiot, no matter how big a mouth he has."

"He's not the only one with a big mouth."

He knew he didn't need to take that kind of shot, but he did it anyway. And it must have landed, because now Anna was quiet.

He said, "Kevin wouldn't have had to figure out anything if you hadn't told him."

"Wow," she said. "Now I'm really starting to feel better."

"I didn't know this was about making you feel better," Charlie said.

"As soon as I get off the phone I'm going to call Gramps."

"And tell him the whole story?"

"Just like I told it to you."

"Make sure you tell him that I would never have told in a million years," Charlie said.

She said she would, she promised.

"You know I'd never purposely do anything to hurt you?" she said. "You do know that, right?"

Charlie felt tired all of a sudden. "I know."

There was a long silence now, both ends of the phone. Neither one of them ever talked just to talk the way Kevin Fallon did. But right now it was just as if there was nothing more to say.

Finally Anna said she'd call after she talked to her grandfather, if she could get him. He sometimes went to bed earlier than they did. Charlie said he was going to hit it himself pretty soon.

"Talk tomorrow, then," she said.

"Okay."

There was a knock on the door, then Charlie saw his mom stepping inside his room, portable house phone in her hand, and a look on her face that in Charlie's whole life had never ever meant anything good, at least not for him.

His mom pointed the phone at him, saying to him, "Is there some reason why I just had to tell a sportswriter from the *Los Angeles Times* that you're not allowed to give interviews on school nights?"

Charlie and his mom were sitting at the kitchen table, Charlie just having told her the whole story. She wasn't a football fan as much as Charlie was, didn't follow it, only cared about it because he cared about it. He'd tried to explain to her why the Bulldogs getting Tom Pinkett was such a smart thing for them to do—there was hardly any risk, it was the same thing he did in fantasy when he had to make a call on a player, risk versus reward.

"It's like some actor who hasn't had a big part in a long time," his mom said. "When he gets a big part, everybody says, 'Where's he been?'"

"Exactly."

It was past ten o'clock by now, his normal bedtime for a school night, even though his mom liked to joke that it was "soft" ten, knowing how many times she had opened the door and found him still on his laptop.

"The reporter actually believed I was going to put you on the phone with him," she said.

"It's because I'm a kid," Charlie said.

"Well, *yeah*."

"I told Anna before, nobody would think this was a story if it had been an adult who'd suggested Tom Pinkett to Mr. Warren."

"It's not just a story," his mom said. "People are going to look at it as a *drama*, especially between Joe Warren and his son."

"All because of me."

"Not all because of you," she said, "which is why we are going to keep you out of this. It's because of Anna and Kevin and Kevin's dad and, guess what, because your friend Mr. Warren actually decided to sign your other friend the quarterback because you told him to. Everybody's got to own this."

"But I didn't *tell* him to!" Charlie said. "All I told him was that I thought the guy could still play."

"So he can handle the fallout, not you," she said. "Hopefully the media will know enough to leave a twelve-year-old boy alone. But no contact with anybody in the media, Charles Christopher Gaines. No Facebook, no Twitter, nothing. Somebody else may choose to keep this drama going. But it's not going to be us."

"I just don't want Mr. Warren to think it was me that started it."

Stuck on that.

"You said Anna was taking care of that."

"The least she could do."

"You know she didn't mean any harm," his mom said. "In an odd way, it was just her way of defending you with Kevin. Try to look at it that way, as hard as that is for you right now."

She had put cookies on a plate between them, even though it was late. Charlie had eaten one, washed it down with a glass of milk. His mom had always told him that cookies and milk could make you feel better about almost anything. In a way, this was the best part of the whole night, the end of it, the two of them sitting here talking.

He wished they were talking about anything else, but still—it had been a long time since they'd sat at the table like this, trying to solve the problems of the universe.

"How do I handle this tomorrow at school?"

"You just try to make a joke out of it, say that everything just got blown out of proportion," she said. "Whatever you do, don't lie. That's something that never changes. It's like I've told you your whole life: The truth is always much easier to remember."

"Okay."

"I wouldn't even mention it on your next podcast," she said. "Because that would be a way of you keeping the story going."

"Nobody listens to my dopey podcast anyway."

"*Really?*" she said, grinning at him.

"If Mr. Warren hadn't thought Tom Pinkett was a good idea, he wouldn't have brought him to the Bulldogs."

"Tell that to your friends."

"Okay," he said again.

"And now go to bed, Mr. General Manager, and let me figure out how I plan to handle this tomorrow if any of your other new friends in the media decide to call me."

"They're not my friends!" Charlie said. "And don't call me Mr. General Manager."

She said she was just trying to lighten the mood, for both of them, even though Charlie could see she wasn't happy with what had happened tonight, telling him when they sat down at the table that it wasn't in her plans to be the parent of a Hollywood child star.

She said she would be up to say good night in a few minutes, told him not to call anybody, not even Anna, that Anna could tell him about her conversation with her grandfather in the morning. Told him to shut off his computer so he wouldn't be tempted to go searching the Net to see what people might be saying. They were officially done for the night, his mom said, and would regroup in the morning.

Charlie did what he was told, went upstairs and washed his face, brushed his teeth, put on a pair of his favorite basketball shorts, and a cool UCLA T-shirt, in that cool UCLA blue, that Anna had gotten him.

He was even more tired than he thought. His eyes were closing for real when his mom came in, kissed him on the forehead, told him she loved him.

"Look at my football man," she said.

"Yeah, look at me."

A couple of minutes after she had shut the door behind her, Charlie heard his phone buzzing on the nightstand next to him. He thought about letting it go to voice mail, but when he looked at the phone this is what he saw:

L.A. Bulldogs.

He picked it up and said in a soft voice, "This is Charlie."

"And this is your friend Joe Warren," he said. "I hope it's not too late to call."

"Not tonight it's not, sir."

"Good."

"Mr. Warren, I am so sorry."

"For what?"

"For all this coming out the way it did about Tom Pinkett and you and Matt."

"I just got off the phone with my extremely apologetic granddaughter," he said. "And I am going to tell you what I told her: chill."

The word sounded funny coming from him.

"But my mom just got a call from a reporter," Charlie said, making sure to keep his voice down.

"Probably the same one who called me. Nice young fella named Bill Spencer. Dad's a columnist in New York. Gil Spencer. Known Gil for years and like him. Most sportswriters are about as fun to deal with as lawyers."

Charlie thinking: How could Mr. Warren be this chill?

"What did you tell him?"

"Why, I told him the truth. Told him I was watching a preseason game with a young man who knows his football and he suggested we give Tom Pinkett a look, and we did, and we're glad we did."

Charlie pulled the covers over himself. "But what about the part about Matt not wanting him?"

"Told him the truth about that, too." Charlie heard the old man laugh. "Told him that we have disagreements all the time about players. HBO could get one of those *Hard Knocks* series just by setting up cameras in our draft room. Also told him that if fair people were keeping score, my son has made a lot more smart decisions than people realize. And has overruled his old man plenty of times when I wanted to make a really dumb decision."

Charlie with the covers over him, talking to the owner of the Bulldogs, about a story that was going to be in the paper about both of them in the morning.

Not sure anymore whether this was a dream or a nightmare or both.

"I'm still sorry it came out like this," Charlie said.

"It's okay, Charlie, really it is. For now, just figure out when you can come back to practice," Joe Warren said. "If that's still all right with your mom, I'll set it up with Carlos."

Charlie said he would.

"Before I hang up, not that you actually hang up one of these toy phones, let me leave you with something, Charlie," Joe Warren said. "It doesn't matter how old or young you are: The truth will always catch up with you eventually. Trust me on that."

"My mom always tells me pretty much the same thing."

"Smart woman," Joe Warren said. "Best thing is to own the truth from the start, whether you like it or not."

Using the same expression—owning it—his mom just had.

Joe Warren said, "Just remember what I'm telling you, Charlie. It's important."

Charlie suddenly wondering if he wanted to talk all night, if he was just settling in the way his granddaughter did sometimes.

There was a brief silence at his end of the phone, like he wanted to say one more thing, but all the old man said was "Night, kid."

Sixteen

THE NEXT MORNING THE FRONT headline of the sports section read like this: KID GM? Beneath it, the article included this quote from Joe Warren:

If they're good ideas, I don't care where they come from.

His son, Charlie saw, took a slightly different approach.

You know what players I'm focused on this week? Matt said in Bill Spencer's story. *I'm focused on our players, and the ones they're going to be lining up against. Which means this week is pretty much like every other week. Everybody else can have their fun. Getting ready for our next game is always mine.*

When Bill Spencer had gone back at Matt Warren about whether the story about Charlie was true or not, Matt had said, *If we continue to have this conversation, we're both going to feel like twelve-year-olds. I didn't ask my dad why he wanted me to take another look at Tom Pinkett. But once he asked, we did our due diligence and decided he might help us. End of story.*

Charlie asked his mother what due diligence was.

"Sort of like homework," she said. "Do you believe Matt Warren didn't ask his dad why he wanted Tom Pinkett all of a sudden?"

"Don't know," Charlie said. "And don't care much right now."

She had asked if Charlie wanted her to drive him to school today, but he said no, there was enough weirdness going on, he'd be happy to be on the bus with his friends.

Yet it turned out the guys on the bus, none of whom actually read the morning paper, had all either read about the story on their phone or had heard from their friends about Charlie and Tom Pinkett.

Pete Ciccone, one of the better baseball players in their grade, said, "Wow, is it true you're calling the shots now with the Dogs?"

"Yeah," Charlie said, trying to take his mom's advice, keep things light. "Next I'm thinking about replacing the head coach."

Then he quickly added, "Just kidding. People are making way more of this than is actually there."

"Not the way it sounded on the TV when I was eating my cereal," Pete said.

"It was on the TV this morning?" Charlie said.

"Just *SportsCenter*," Pete said. "Nothing major," he added with a grin.

"*Awesome*," Charlie said, shaking his head, staring down at his sneakers. "*Truly* awesome."

Anna was waiting for him in front of the school, no sign of Kevin Fallon, Charlie still not sure how he was going to handle that one. He just wanted to believe that Kevin didn't want to turn

Charlie's life sideways any more than Anna did, that both of them had gotten into a dumb game of who knew more.

"You believe how big this has gotten this fast?" Charlie said.

"I kind of do, actually," she said. "And you might not want to hear this, especially from me, but it's not like it's the end of the world as we know it."

"Feels like it."

"Oh, *come on*," she said. "You're famous. Get over it."

He looked at her, all tough girl now, maybe done apologizing for everything. Going back to being Anna.

"Get over it?" Charlie said. "I'm sorry, did I do something wrong here?"

"Did I do something wrong by helping you become famous?" Anna said. "Yeah, get over it, Gaines."

He didn't say anything, mostly because she'd nailed it. And nailed him in the process. She wasn't right as often as she thought she was—nobody could possibly be. But she was right this time. There *was* a part of him that didn't hate this. He still didn't want to cause trouble for Anna's grandfather, or her uncle. He genuinely felt bad that this had gotten out the way it had. But for once, Charlie wasn't just Brain, wasn't just the football nerd guy.

He could see it with his classmates on the bus, even the ones he didn't consider close friends: They were treating him differently today. Not like the child star that his mom had talked about the night before.

Just a star.

That was another truth he didn't want to outrun, that he wasn't afraid to own, even if he wasn't going to tell Anna.

Both their buses had arrived at school early today. So they had some time before the bell rang, went and sat in the grass near the front entrance.

"Your gramps said he had a good talk with you," Charlie said, trying to change the subject at least a little bit.

"He called you? He said he was going to. You guys have a good talk?"

"They're all good talks with him."

Anna said, "Yeah, he's totally cool with the whole thing, just like he always is. It's my mom whose head nearly exploded."

Anna explained that after she'd called her grandfather she'd told her mom what had happened. And that her mom had lit into her, saying that if Anna hadn't been talking about family business with Kevin, none of this would have happened.

"My mom's big on family," Anna said. "Even bigger on the family business."

Putting air quotes around family business.

"She said that it didn't matter what I thought of the job my uncle Matt was doing, he's the general manager of the team, and not me. And for me to stay out of his business."

"But you just said it's a family business."

"Everybody in the family except me today." She turned and looked at him. "What about your mom?"

"Still not happy about a reporter calling and interrupting the episode of *Scandal* she missed last week."

Anna said, "That's probably why my mom said she wanted to talk to your mom after we were at school."

"That's never good."

"Sounds like they might want to be unhappy with the two of us together."

Charlie checked his phone. Five minutes to the opening bell.

"This is going to go away, right?" he said.

"Yeah," Anna said. "But maybe not as soon as we want it to."

"Let's just try to get through the day, and get me to football practice, without making any more trouble."

Anna said that sounded like a plan to her.

It worked for the rest of the school day, even when Kevin joined them for lunch, asking Charlie about ten different ways how he could make up for this before Charlie told him that if he didn't stop apologizing, then he was really going to get mad.

"I didn't know what I didn't know," Kevin said.

"Happens to the best of us," Charlie said.

"You're a better friend than I am."

Charlie said, "Not keeping score, dude."

The rest of the day Charlie handled the jokes and teasing going from class to class, actually started to feel like maybe this really wasn't the worst thing that had ever happened to anybody, everybody looking at him differently, Charlie really not hating being treated like some kind of star.

Then he and Anna came walking out of school after the closing bell and saw the television trucks in front of Culver City Middle.

A first.

Both of them knowing who the trucks—and the reporters standing in front of them—were here for, a hundred percent.

"Really?" Anna said.

"Really," Charlie said.

Then they turned right around and walked back into school and did the only thing they could do in an emergency like this:

Whipped out their cell phones and called their moms.

"This isn't going to improve their mood," Anna said.

"Not even a little bit."

The highlight in front of the school, Charlie decided on the ride home, his mom driving and Mrs. Bretton sitting next to her, was when Mrs. Bretton first got out of the car.

She walked up to the reporters standing on the street, didn't bother to introduce herself, and said, "I hope you all understand that if either of our children get so much as a camera pointed in their direction, your satellite trucks might end up parking in Encino for Bulldogs games. You do get that, right?"

Not raising her voice, or acting mad. Even smiling as she said it.

One of the reporters was a blond woman who Anna said looked like she could have been a Bulldogs' cheerleader once.

She said to Anna's mom, "And who are you exactly, ma'am?"

The mean look, all big eyes, that Anna would put on Charlie sometimes—he now knew who she got it from.

"Don't *ma'am* me," Mrs. Bretton said. "My married name is Bretton. That probably won't mean much to you. But my maiden name is Warren. As in Joe Warren. As in my dad. As in the owner of the team."

"We didn't mean to upset anybody," the blond reporter said. "We just all think this is kind of a cute story."

"You want a cute story? I think a panda is about to be born at the San Diego Zoo. If you catch a break on the 405, maybe you can all make it down there before they close."

Charlie's mom took it from there.

"I am Charlie Gaines's mom," she said. "He's twelve and when he left for school today, he wasn't looking to get into show business beyond his very entertaining new podcast. And he's certainly not looking to get into show business now. So back off, okay?"

She stood there with her hands on her hips, looking at all the reporters at once and said, "We done here?"

"Yes, m . . . Mrs. Gaines," one of the male reporters said, barely stopping himself from ma'am-ing Charlie's mom, probably afraid that one of the moms would take his microphone away and hit him over the head with it.

Charlie's mom took his hand, Anna's mom took hers, they got into the car and Charlie's mom drove away.

"*That*," Anna said, "was pretty cool."

"Zip it, missy," her mom said, whipping her head around from the front seat.

"Mom," she said, "I was just trying to give you some props."

"Thanks," her mom said. "But what part of 'zip it' didn't you get, daughter of mine?"

"The two mothers in this car have already had a long talk about this," Karla Gaines said. "And we are in perfect agreement that the two of you have to make sure that you don't do anything to keep driving this story, or draw any more attention to yourselves."

"Mom," Charlie said, "we didn't go looking for attention. It wasn't like I called a press conference or anything."

"My father and brother are the ones who are going to do that," Anna's mom said.

"They're calling a press conference?" Charlie said. "Because of *this*?"

"They figure they need to put a stop to this now," Anna's mom said. "And they think the best way to do it is to tackle it head-on. And then hope it goes away."

"But you do understand that Charlie had nothing to do with any of this, right, Mom?" Anna said.

"Doesn't matter," Charlie's mom said. "Charlie's the one who's out there. And it doesn't just involve him, it involves your family, too."

"And that," Mrs. Bretton said, "is why the two of you are going to help by not saying another word about this that could end up in the media. Which to the two of you means social media. Got it?"

"Got it," Charlie and Anna said, like they were using the same voice.

It happened a lot, good times and bad. Like they were thinking the same thoughts.

"All I'm going to try to do is have a good practice with the Car-dinals," Charlie said. "They're the only team I'm going to worry about for the rest of the day."

He meant it, too. Meant it when they dropped Anna and her mom off, meant it all the way into his pads and to Memorial Field.

It just wasn't the way things worked out.

Seventeen

ALWAYS, FROM THE TIME CHARLIE had become the kind of sports fan that he was, he had read and heard the same thing from athletes: No matter what was happening to them off the field, they could find shelter—or refuge, or peace—on the field.

It was what he had been looking forward to at the end of this day, after all the craziness of the last twenty-four hours. Even if it hadn't been twenty-four hours since Mr. Fallon, whether he'd meant to or not, had turned Charlie into the most famous seventh grader in Los Angeles.

It was Sean Barkley, the guy on the team who did even more talking than Kevin Fallon, who started in on Charlie as soon as they were on the field stretching.

"Hey," Sean said in a loud voice to his teammates, "you think *our* QB has to worry about his job now that Gaines gets to decide who plays QB for the Bulldogs? What's up with that, Jarrod, you feel like you got to be watchin' your back?"

Jarrod Benedict said, "I think I'll be fine."

Usually Sean Barkley was funny, not trying to sound mean,

had even been giving Charlie props ever since he'd spotted that formation against Redondo Beach and set Sean up for the interception that had saved the game. But today it was Charlie's turn to be on the receiving end of Sean's chirp, Charlie telling himself to make sure he laughed along with everybody else, whether he thought it was funny or not. Not wanting to be the guy who thought everything was funny until it was about him.

"You hearing this, Coach?" Sean said.

"I think people in Tijuana are hearing you, Sean, as a matter of fact," Coach said. "Maybe people in outer space."

"Coach," Sean said, "I'm just worried Gaines here might branch out, tell you to put somebody else besides me at wide-out when you give me a chance to play offense. Or have somebody else covering the other team's best wide-out, like I usually do so brilliantly."

"I think you'll be fine, Sean, really I do," Coach said, grinning.

Charlie'd always thought it was as if Sean Barkley was trying to model himself after Charles Barkley on television. Or maybe thought the two of them were distant relatives.

"Why don't we just get ready to play now, Sean," Jarrod Benedict said, but couldn't resist adding, "I am still playing, right, Charlie?"

That got a laugh out of most of the Cardinals, making Charlie think it was all right to join in.

"Long as you keep winning, JB," Charlie said.

Thinking—hoping—that might get everybody to move on to something else.

Like maybe football.

As the players were strapping on their helmets, Coach came over and put an arm around Charlie.

"You okay with Sean busting your chops a little?" Coach said.

Charlie said, "I didn't think I had much of a choice."

Coach Dayley walked him away from the other players and said, "Lot of football coaches think they're deep thinkers, Charlie. From Pop Warner right up through the NFL. But I'm not one of them."

Charlie not sure where he was going with this.

"I'll never know as much about the game as you do, Coach," he said.

"I'm not talking about football right now," Coach Dayley said. "I'm talking about how we're all supposed to live our lives when there's no game going on."

Charlie waited.

"What I'm trying to tell you," Coach said, "is that it doesn't matter who you are or how young or old you are, eventually it's going to be your turn to stand alone onstage."

"Onstage?"

"Just an expression, Charlie. A way of telling you that when it's your turn, you may have to take a different kind of hit than you do on the football field, and there's not a darn thing you can do about it."

Coach Dayley blew his whistle then, yelled at the rest of the team to gather at midfield. They'd had their fun with Charlie today, now it was time to have bigger fun, which to him always meant hitting somebody.

"Can I ask you something?" Charlie said to Coach Dayley as the two of them walked to midfield.

"Shoot."

"How do I get off the stage?"

Coach smiled, banged a fist on Charlie's right shoulder pad.

"You just have to wait until it's somebody else's turn."

It turned out to be a really good practice, lots of good plays on both sides of the ball, Charlie even making a couple of solid tackles.

One of them came with just a few minutes left, Coach Dayley having announced that the offense would get three more downs to try to score. Sean Barkley moved back to offense by then, Coach using him as a third wide receiver the way he did sometimes in games.

And on the second-to-last play of the day, the offense went with one of Coach's versions of the end around, Jarrod pitching the ball to Sean.

Who thought he was as good and fast with the ball in his hands as Kevin Fallon was, even though everybody on the Cardinals knew better. Sean was good. And he was fast. Just not as good and fast as Kevin.

Most of the guys on D had taken the bait when Jarrod faked a handoff to Kevin, getting ready to chase him the way they usually did. So somehow Charlie ended up alone in the right flat with Sean Barkley—who was a lot faster and better than Charlie Gaines—coming right at him.

Charlie figured Sean wouldn't try to run him over, that wasn't his style, he thought he had more moves in the open field than LeBron James had in the open court.

So there was only one question for Charlie to answer, in the moment:

Inside or outside?

Sean was the one who made the first move, a little lean to his right, to the outside, dropping his shoulder.

But in that moment Charlie outthought one of the best players on their team. He knew this wasn't just a little bit of a head-and-shoulder fake, that Sean really was planning to go that way, take it to the outside and then all the way to the house, that he planned to end practice right now, by running right past Charlie Gaines.

Who read the move and read the play the way real linebackers did in moments like this, when they were the ones out there alone.

Moving to his left as Sean took a big step to his right, doing what the coaches always told him to do, making himself as wide as possible while staying as low to the ground as possible. Keeping himself in front of Sean and giving him no room to get to the sideline.

Then dropping his own shoulder and wrapping his arms around Sean's legs, doing that as he drove him back.

Before he just buried him.

The next thing he heard, still on top of Sean Barkley, was Coach blowing his whistle again and saying, "You know what, boys? I think we'll just go ahead and end today with a lick like that."

Charlie rolled off Sean, got to his feet first. And even after the way practice had ended, extended a hand to help him up.

Not sure how Sean would handle it.

But Sean just reached up, smiling, took Charlie's hand, and let out a low whistle and said, "Look at Brain. Taking me down."

And this time it was Charlie who couldn't resist talking.

"Wasn't my brain that put you down, Sean," he said. "That was just *me*."

A little chirp from the kid onstage.

Eighteen

FOR ONCE AT DINNER CHARLIE got to talk about his own football, not somebody else's, telling his mom all about his tackle on Sean, telling her what he said after Sean called him Brain.

When she asked Charlie how his teammates were reacting to what she called his sudden fame, he told her that there'd been some jokes and chop-busting, but that mostly they were cool with him. And that he was cool with them.

Which he really was, thinking that it hadn't been all that bad and could have been much worse if the Cardinals weren't as close as they were.

"So what could have been a rough day wasn't," his mom said.

"Not gonna lie, Mom," he said. "I felt like The Man making that tackle."

"I still can't believe that the Warrens feel as if they need to hold a press conference," she said.

"Anna says it was mostly her uncle's idea, because he thinks he's the one taking the most heat. But he sincerely does think it's the best way for everybody to move on and get past this. Her uncle

Matt told her mom that it doesn't take much for little things to become big things in sports. Especially in L.A."

"Not just sports," she said. "But even understanding what everybody on the outside sees in the entertainment value of all this, I'm with good old Uncle Matt: Let's move on."

"But you still think it's all right for me to think there's a fun factor to all this?" Charlie said.

"Honey, it's perfectly all right. You're twelve and an instant celebrity and you have a right to feel like this is an adventure. But I also don't want the TV trucks showing up in front of our house now that they came to your school."

"You were great at school."

"Not gonna lie to *you*," she said. "That did feel pretty good."

"Like me taking down Sean?"

They both laughed. Then his mom held up a finger and said, "Just remember the rules about not becoming Mr. Social Network."

"I know them better than my homework."

He went upstairs then, did what little homework he had on this night. When he was finished he took a deep breath, opened up Google, typed in *Charlie Gaines*, felt his eyes getting big as he saw how many hits there were.

Tried to decide if he wanted to keep going.

A writer he liked a lot had spoken at Culver City Middle School when he was on a book tour last year and said he never Googled his name to see what people were saying about him. When Anna— of course, Anna—raised a hand and wanted to know why, the writer said, "If I don't know them, why should I care about what they only think they know about me?"

But the writer wasn't twelve and feeling like his life was like some ride at Disneyland all of a sudden.

So he read some of the stories written by people who didn't know him, discovered that nobody was picking on him, they were mostly having fun with Mr. Warren and Matt. Some of it was pretty mean, he had to admit, Charlie figuring it would be even worse if the Bulldogs hadn't played as well as they had in their opening two games.

And—much more important—if Tom Pinkett hadn't been playing as well as *he* had.

One NFC West blogger at ESPN.com said that if the Bulldogs were going to let a boy wizard call the shots, wouldn't they have been better off just going with Harry Potter?

Later on in the same story the guy wrote:

I was always a sucker for stories about boys and their dogs when I was a boy. I just never thought I'd grow up to hear one involving a boy and the L.A. Bulldogs.

Charlie had to admit that wasn't too bad.

He finally stopped reading when he got to a story that said if this was all true, Mr. Warren was acting like a "desperate old fool resorting to publicity stunts as a way of somehow keeping his team relevant." That one was on an NFL website Charlie had never heard of, and he thought he'd heard of almost all of them.

So he did stop reading, then closed his laptop like he was closing out the rest of the world. He thought about calling Anna, knowing she'd still be up. But also knowing you couldn't be tired and hold up your end of the conversation with Anna Bretton.

And Charlie was tired.

Like he had spent a whole entire twenty-four hours at Disneyland, going from one ride to another without stopping, the way he did when he was little.

On his bed now, hands behind his head.

But how much fun was he having, really?

He'd always thought Anna was luckier than he was. Not only because her family owned an NFL team, but because she had such a big family. She had her mom and her dad and an older brother and sister, both of them in college. Then came Anna's gramps and her uncle.

When Anna's brother and sister were in town, the Brettons and Warrens were all together at Bulldogs home games.

Like every one of those Sundays was a family reunion.

Charlie's family reunions?

Him and his mom at dinner.

And he had to admit, seeing Anna's family from the inside this way, seeing how her uncle Matt in particular was reacting to everything, Charlie wasn't so sure now if Anna had it as good as he'd always thought she did.

His mom chose that moment to come in and say good night to him.

"Wow," she said, "didn't even have to tell you lights-out tonight."

"I'm a whupped dog," he said.

"A whupped L.A. Bulldog?" she said.

"Good one, Mom," he said, adding, "Love you."

"Loved you first."

He thought he would go right to sleep, but didn't, head still spinning with everything going on, good and bad. So he was still awake when he heard the buzzing from his phone on his bedside table that meant a text, incoming.

Didn't reach over for the phone at first, thinking it had to be from Anna. But then worried it might be from a reporter who'd somehow gotten his number. Hoping it wasn't. Because if it was from a reporter he'd have to go and tell his mom, because he'd promised her that he would.

Charlie reached over, saw that it was a blocked number.

If it was from a reporter, nothing he could do about it, didn't mean he had to respond, just had to report to Mom.

Only it wasn't from a reporter.

Charlie: Hope this isn't too late. And hope you don't mind. Got your number from Mr. Warren. Just wanted to say thanks for the faith. Tom Pinkett.

The phone call came right after that, from Mr. Warren. Asking Charlie if he could talk to his mom.

Nineteen

THE CARTOON WAS IN THE sports section of the *Los Angeles Times* that morning, Charlie's mom saying he might as well see it before he went to school. And pointing out that the *Times* hardly ever ran cartoons anywhere except on the editorial page.

"If it wasn't about you, it would actually be kind of amusing," she said.

"But it is about me," Charlie said.

"That it is."

The boy in the cartoon was identified as "Charlie," but looked almost exactly like Charlie Brown in the Christmas TV special that was one of Charlie Gaines's favorites when he was little.

But the Charlie in the *Times* was a puppet master, pulling strings for cartoon figures of Joe and Matt Warren, the two of them flopping in midair above Bulldogs Stadium.

"Well, I have to say they have made you look adorable," his mom said.

"But it's not me," he said. "And the Warrens aren't going to be happy."

He groaned.

"I went to bed feeling good," he said. "But now I'm feeling bad about this all over again."

His mom patted his hand.

"Fame is a cruel mistress," she said.

"Is that supposed to be funny?" Charlie said.

That was the way the day started.

Now Charlie was waiting for the Bulldogs' press conference to begin. It was being held in the interview room underneath Bulldogs Stadium, the same one they used for the coaches and players after games.

Matt Warren stepped to the microphone at exactly four o'clock, Joe Warren behind him.

"Ladies and gentlemen, thank you for coming," Matt said, "to what is probably the most unusual gathering that we've ever had here. But then my dad and I just felt that it was the best way to handle an unusual situation.

"There has been so much speculation over the past day and a half about our new quarterback, Tom Pinkett, that we decided to just clear the air, set the record straight, and move on to what we feel are slightly more important matters—like, oh I don't know, the rest of the season."

Joe Warren, who didn't have a microphone, nodded and said, "In no particular order," and smiled himself when he heard some of the people in the audience laugh.

Matt laughed, too.

"Sometimes my dad and I get the idea that you guys don't think we can laugh at ourselves," Matt said. "But we can." He looked out at the media crowd. "We manage to have fun around here, even though losing is never fun. But when the fun stops, we go back to doing what we always do in this organization, and that means making decisions that we think are in the best interests of the organization. And think you'd all agree that we made the right call bringing in Tom Pinkett to compete for the quarterback job, and ultimately win it, off what he's shown so far," Matt said.

Matt Warren clearly didn't really want to be here or doing this, but Charlie thought he was acting cool about the whole thing. Certainly not acting like some kind of cartoon puppet.

"What I want you all to know is that there's no controversy here," Matt said, "the way there's no controversy about bringing Tom to the Bulldogs in the first place." He smiled. "And no more family drama than we usually have around here."

He turned and said, "Right, Dad?"

"Well," Joe Warren said, "not like the kind they have in that family where the girls keep marrying basketball players and I keep wondering why Bruce Jenner looks the way he does."

Got an even bigger laugh this time.

The Bulldogs' PR man, Greg Arguello, whom Charlie had met at practice, stepped to the microphone now.

"Okay, Matt and Joe will take a few questions," Greg said.

A reporter in the first row who introduced herself as being from Fox 1 said, "Matt, is it true that the Bulldogs originally brought Tom Pinkett here against your wishes? And is it also true that the idea about Tom came from a twelve-year-old friend of your niece?"

Matt Warren managed to keep smiling. "If you ask my niece, she doesn't think any of this would have happened without her."

"Tell me about it," Charlie said to his mom.

"Anna will be *so* pleased," Karla Gaines said.

The Fox 1 woman said, "So you're not embarrassed?"

Matt Warren was ready for that one. "My dad always told me that the problem with a good idea is that once it gets inside your head, you can never get it out. No matter how it gets in there. That's how we all feel about Tom Pinkett."

Now a reporter Charlie recognized, Sal Paolantonio from ESPN, stood up.

"So, Matt, you didn't have to get talked into this, is that what you're saying?"

"Neither my dad nor I ever has to be talked into something that has a chance to improve our team. If you ever came up with a good idea, we'd even listen to you, Sal."

Now Matt Warren was the one in the family getting a laugh.

But the guy known as Sal Pal wasn't backing off.

"So you're saying that almost anybody can make personnel decisions now with the Bulldogs?"

"Sal," Matt Warren, still keeping his cool, "I don't think we're going to start polling all the middle schools in Los Angeles when next year's draft rolls around. Listen, my dad used to love to play the horses at Santa Anita. And believe me, he'd take tips from guys in the hot dog line if he thought they were giving him a winner."

"There *are* a lot of smart people in those lines," Joe Warren said.

Charlie didn't know how much of this Joe and Matt Warren had prepared. But it was working for them. Like he and Matt had an act.

Sal Paolantonio took one more run at Matt.

"Matt, I'm sure you saw the *Times* today. You're telling me you're not at all bothered that you're being portrayed as a puppet?"

"Sal, the only thing that bothered me is that I thought I looked a little fat," Matt said. "First thing I said to my dad this morning was, 'You think I look fat in this cartoon?'"

Joe Warren said, "I told my son that while I love him very much, yes, the cartoon did make it look as if he could lose a few pounds."

"One last question, one I'm asking for a lot of local football fans," Sal said. "Who's really running the Los Angeles Bulldogs?"

"The same people who've run them from day one," Matt said.

Smile gone now. Suddenly it was as if he and Sal Paolantonio were the only two people in the room.

"You sure about that, Matt?"

"Well, as sure as you were when you picked us to go 4–12 this season."

"This isn't about me, Matt."

"*You* sure?"

Greg Arguello leaned in front of Matt Warren now, said, "I'm sorry, Sal, but when did this turn into one of those debate shows on your network?"

Before Sal could answer, Joe Warren took over.

Put a shaky hand out, made his way between his son and his PR man, stepped to the microphone himself.

"Sal," he said, "the Bulldogs are, and always have been, my team. My son, in whom I have great trust and confidence, ultimately works for me the way the coach does, the players, the scouts. And the groundskeepers. It's always been that way. I'm an old-fashioned guy who likes old-fashioned expressions, so here's one that explains all that: It's still my nickel. You want to come at somebody, come at me."

Then Joe turned to Matt and said, "You think it's time to bring out the one they really want to be talking to?"

"Absolutely," Matt said.

He turned and looked over his shoulder. There were curtains over there. It was where one player waited while another one was being interviewed after games.

"Charlie," Matt said, "why don't you come out here so all these nice people can meet you."

Charlie's mom, behind the curtain with him, where they'd been all along, the two of them watching the press conference on the television back there, said, "Go get 'em, big boy."

She pulled back the curtain.

At first Charlie just poked his head out, as every reporter and photographer turned his way, and he heard people shouting his name and saw all the TV cameras pointed right at him.

"Charlie!"

"Charlie, over here!"

"Smile, Charlie!"

Charlie came all the way out now, looked across at Joe Warren, who winked at him, motioned for him to come over to the stage.

"Meet our new special assistant, Charlie Gaines," Joe Warren announced into the microphone.

Twenty

AFTER SUPPER, CHARLIE'S MOM DROPPED him off in town; Anna's mom did the same with her.

They tried to make things seem the way they always were on a night like this, first going to Cold Stone and then taking their ice cream to the park, crowded on this night, their usual bench taken, having to walk around for a little bit before they found an empty one.

Both of them knowing that things were definitely *not* the same as they'd always been, probably weren't going to be anytime soon.

Not exactly the football season I expected, Charlie kept thinking.

Anna said, "I thought I came off very well today, if we're focusing on the positives."

"No kidding. Your uncle made it sound as if you practically had to take me by the hand to your grandfather so I could tell him what I thought about Tom Pinkett."

"Got a problem?" Anna said.

Then she said, "You gonna finish your ice cream?"

Charlie said, "Is that ever a serious question with you?"

She reached over for his cup and spoon and finished what he hadn't eaten of Oreo Overload. Somehow Anna Bretton seemed to be able to eat all day long and stay skinny. One more mystery about her. Sometimes Charlie thought that what he knew about her wasn't nearly as interesting as what he didn't.

"You know what might be the most amazing part of the whole day?" Anna said after she'd tossed Charlie's cup into a trash bin. "That your mom even let you go to the press conference!"

"That one is on your gramps, totally," Charlie said. "He can be pretty persuasive, I guess, when he wants to be."

"My mom says he wants people to think his head is full of the sky half the time; that's the way she puts it. And I know he can look like a total frail. But the old guy can still get it done."

On the phone with Charlie's mom after Charlie had gotten the text from Tom Pinkett, Joe Warren told her that the genie was officially out of the bottle—his words—and that the media wasn't going away, they knew they had a good thing with the story of the old owner and the seventh grader, and they were going to be like dogs with bones.

He told her that the only way to deal with it was to deal with it head-on, have Charlie make a surprise appearance at the press conference.

Mr. Warren said they might as well just go ahead and put Charlie's face on the whole thing, so people could stop speculating; the media fed on speculation almost as much as it did on gossip.

"My son will help us set it up" was the way Mr. Warren put it to her. "Then we'll bring out yours for the big finish."

Then he spelled out for her what he already had for Charlie, just in different words.

"Why can't we have some fun with this?" he'd said on the phone. "Can't a geezer like me do that?"

Then, according to Charlie's mom, he told her that a little attention wasn't going to ruin the boy's life, girls would have plenty of time to do that later.

Anna smiled now in the park and said, "He tells me the same thing about boys all the time."

Then she told Charlie that she'd been thinking about it all day, but her favorite part of the press conference was when Greg Arguello had to bring up a chair for Charlie to stand on so he could see over the podium and actually reach the microphone.

"Thanks," Charlie said, rolling his eyes.

Charlie hadn't been at the microphone long when Greg Arguello told the reporters they were going to be limited to a few questions.

The first one came from somebody who said he was from Yahoo Sports, wanting to know what Charlie had seen in Tom Pinkett that nobody else had.

"Numbers," Charlie said, surprised he could get the word out, his mouth feeling as dry as dirt.

At that point he felt like everybody in the room had shouted the same thing at once: "Louder!"

"Sorry," he said.

Mr. Warren reached over, adjusted the microphone one more time to get it closer to him.

"My friend Charlie will get better at this when he's hosting his own talk show," Joe Warren said.

"Actually, Mr. Warren, I already am."

That got Charlie *his* first laugh of the day, even though he was still way behind the old man.

Watching the replay on TV later, Charlie saw the shocked look on his own face, all of these grown-ups actually laughing at something he'd said.

Something else he saw? How happy he looked, the spotlight on him this way. He knew why, too. Once he got out there, and got over his nerves, something that happened faster than he thought it would, he felt good.

Very good.

Mr. Warren slapped his forehead at that point, leaned into the microphone, and said, *"The Charlie Show.* Completely forgot." Grinned and said, "Check your local listings for times."

Charlie thinking at the time that it was like they'd worked out a little act to follow the one everybody had seen from Joe and Matt Warren. But it wasn't an act. It was just happening, the way everything else was these days.

Joe Warren said to Charlie, "Continue, please. Explain to the nice people about Tom Pinkett the way you did to me. Just go a little slower for them."

Charlie pretended he was explaining it to the reporters and cameras the way he would to his fantasy buddies. About how if you looked at the games he'd played all the way back to the Titans, made one sixteen-game season out of them, he was playing at a higher level than when he'd come out of college.

He explained that he always liked to look at what he called MPT—Meaningful Playing Time—and project what a bench guy like Tom could do if he were getting as much MPT as the big boys did at quarterback.

Sal Paolantonio got back up now, and said, "Kid, are you sure you're only twelve?"

Then somebody asked when Charlie was taping the next *Charlie Show*. Charlie said he'd have to check with his producer, and got another laugh.

"He is referring to that granddaughter of mine that my son referenced earlier," Joe Warren said. "Just so you know, she's kind of a hot pistol, too, when it comes to the subject of the L.A. Bulldogs. She and Charlie are a team."

Bill Spencer of the *Los Angeles Times* finally directed the last question of the day at Joe Warren.

"Joe," he said, "you're always saying that this season is the one when the Bulldogs finally make the grade. Have you been referring to *middle* grade?"

"Ladies and gentleman, I can't top a line like that," Joe Warren said. "Thank you for coming. And remember: be nice."

Then he'd helped Charlie down off his chair and the two of them had walked through the curtain.

Now Charlie and Anna were here in the park, Charlie saying to her, "Your uncle is really okay with this?"

"Probably not," she said. "But I have to say, he showed me

something today, not losing his temper, because he's got one. It couldn't have been easy for him being a part of that. Not his style. He'd rather be in some dark room looking at film. But even when Sal Pal came at him, I thought he handled himself great."

"Same," Charlie said.

"But nobody had a better time than Gramps," Anna said. "He took something that people acted like was this big embarrass-ment . . ."

"Meaning me," Charlie said.

She nodded. "Handing out advice to the owner of the team and the general manager. Yeah, he took that and somehow made it a good thing."

"Like he told my mom he would."

"Tell you what about Gramps," Anna said. "He wants people to think he's all shy and everything. But he likes having the spotlight on him. Maybe it's because he's lived his whole life in Los Angeles, but I think he likes to think of himself as some kind of showman. My mom does, too."

"He gets off some pretty good lines," Charlie said, "even though he acts like he's not trying to."

"Mom calls him an old ham to his face," she said. "Then Gramps always comes back at her and says she's got the wrong lunch meat, most Bulldog fans think he's just an old turkey."

They sat silently for a few minutes, watching all the life in the park, all the people, Charlie wondering how many of them cared about the Bulldogs or what had happened at Bulldogs Stadium earlier in the day.

Anna said, "My mom said the best part of the day for her was watching Gramps and Uncle Matt work things out this way, with the spotlight on both of them. But I guess that's what fathers and sons always do in the end, right? Figure it out."

She must have heard what she was saying as soon as the words were out of her mouth, hovering in the air between them.

"Well, that just made me sound dumber than a sock drawer," she said.

"Forget it," Charlie said. "You're totally right. It's what dads do with their sons. Real dads, anyway."

They were quiet for what felt like a long time, until Anna brightened and said that tomorrow's *Charlie Show* was going to be the best yet.

"I am kind of on a roll," he said. "I mean, I could have choked my brains out today, but I thought I crushed it."

She stared at him now. Serious look on her face.

"Easy there, big time," she said.

"C'mon, how about when I was telling Sal Pal from ESPN all about how I evaluated Tom Pinkett?"

She didn't say anything now. Still staring. One eyebrow raised.

"What?"

"Nothing," she said.

"You've got that look."

"No," she said, "I don't. I know you think you know me as well as I know you. But you don't. So stop trying."

"You sound like you're some kind of course I should take in school," he said.

"If you knew me as well as you think you do, you'd know what I'm thinking, but you don't."

"And you're not going to tell me."

"If I wanted to share, I'd share."

Then she reached into the back pocket of her jeans shorts, got out her phone, said her mom would be there in ten to pick them both up.

"Pretty amazing day for you, all around," she said, and then before Charlie could respond, she hit him with one of her short punches to his shoulder and said, "You're welcome, by the way."

Then she ran across the park, daring him to catch her, both of them knowing he couldn't, Charlie feeling the same way he always did with Anna, that not only was he a couple of steps behind now—he was always going to be.

Twenty-One

THE CULVER CITY CARDINALS BEAT Santa Monica on Saturday morning and as good as that news was, the better news was that it could not have happened without the contributions of Charlie Gaines.

Not because of what he did on the field, even though he played more than he usually did and was in on three tackles before half-time. A half like that would have been enough to send him home feeling pretty good about himself—so much better than he ever thought he would this season—if that was his entire contribution to the Cardinals on this day.

But he did even more this time as Assistant Coach Gaines. With four minutes left in the game, Culver City and Santa Monica tied 13–all, Jarrod Benedict had just missed Sean Barkley, who was wide open in the middle of the field, and now the Cardinals were facing fourth-and-ten, getting ready to punt from midfield.

Charlie was standing next to Coach Dayley by then.

"Coach, you always tell me to tell you if I notice something," Charlie said. "Well, I did."

Coach was about to send the rest of the punting team on the field, but there was an official's time-out because the defensive back who'd been covering Sean was still down on the field, holding his right hand, having fallen awkwardly breaking up the play.

"What you got?" Coach said.

Charlie told him that Santa Monica had come hard with nine guys trying to block the Cardinals' last two punts, and had nearly gotten the last one. Both times they had flooded the outside, Charlie noticing how open the middle of the line looked.

"You've got my attention," Coach Dayley said.

"I believe if we short-snapped the ball to our up guy, he could run the middle of the field right past everybody," Charlie said.

"Love it. But who? They'd notice if we stuck Kevin or Sean in there."

"Nick's fast enough," Charlie said. "He only needs one hole to pick up the first down."

Nick Tierney, the Cards' fullback, a better blocker than runner, not that fast out of the blocks. But once he got going, he was tough to bring down in the open field, built more like a tight end.

Coach Dayley said, "A fake punt, tie game, four minutes left? That's your blueprint for success today?"

"Pretty much," Charlie said.

"Well, like old Herm Edwards used to say when he was coaching the Jets," Coach Dayley said. "You play to win the game."

Coach grabbed Nick and told him what they were going to do. Told him to tell their center and to tell the rest of the guys in the offensive line to block like they were blocking for a punt, and push to the outside.

"Sort of hoping you and I are right here, Charlie," Coach Dayley said to Charlie in a low voice.

"*Sort of?*" Charlie said. "I can't even breathe."

Their punter lined up as normal, ten yards behind the long snapper. The ball was snapped. But instead of the ball going to the punter, it landed right in the hands of Nick Tierney, who paused just long enough to allow the punter to fake the kick as the linemen on both teams settled into their blocks. Then Nick shot right up the middle and into the open field, made the best open field move Nick Tierney had ever made in his life, and dropped the last guy with a chance to tackle him, Santa Monica's punt returner. Nick ran the rest of the way untouched, into the end zone for the score that would end up winning the game for the Cardinals.

Charlie stayed where he was, watching Nick run the play out, but, Coach Dayley ended up thirty yards down the sideline, cheering Nick on the whole way. When he came back, out of breath, he put a bear hug on Charlie and lifted him into the air.

The good times got even better the next day when the Bulldogs won again, 27–24 against the Jets. Tom Pinkett led the Dogs down the field with under a minute left and no time-outs, completing the game-winning pass to Harrison Mays in the right corner of the end zone with six seconds left.

On Monday, Carlos, Mr. Warren's driver, picked Charlie up from school and drove him to practice. Charlie had asked Anna to go with him, but she had soccer practice.

This time they didn't go down to the field, just sat in Mr. Warren's office, the small deck behind it looking down on the practice field.

Talking football. Bulldogs football.

What else?

"We'll just stay here today," the old man said. "We gave them enough of a photo op the other day."

Charlie said, "It seemed like you had a good time the other day, though."

"Not gonna lie, Charlie boy, this season looks like it might provide more fun to an old man than he ever thought possible."

"Yesterday was as good as we've looked in a long time."

"Starts with the fact that we've finally got ourselves a real live QB."

Charlie said, "It's more than that, Mr. Warren. Look at all the stops we made on defense when we had to, especially in the fourth quarter."

"Yeah, Coach Fiore tried to explain why when it was over, all about his cover two and all the rest of it. But when he goes all inside football on me, I just tell him how happy I am that we're finally covering *somebody*."

"I love inside football," Charlie said. "And outside football. My mom says I dream in Xs and Os."

"Matt was like that," Joe Warren said. "But he was more interested in playing when he was your age."

"I like playing, too."

"Anna tells me you're better than you like to let on," the old man said.

This was a noncontact day for the Bulldogs, but they were still going through plays, Tom throwing the ball as well as he had the day before. He'd said to the sideline reporter after the game that he'd forgotten what it was like to throw that kind of pass to win the game.

"The great quarterbacks, they get to do it all the time, feels like," he'd said. "Been a while for me. But maybe you can teach an old dog new tricks."

"You mean teach an old Bulldog new tricks, don't you?" the woman had said.

The only bad part of the victory had been the Bulldogs losing their Pro Bowl middle linebacker, Oradell Monroe, in the fourth quarter with what turned out to be a torn ACL. He was scheduled to undergo surgery the next day and would be out for the rest of the season.

On the field below them Oradell's replacement, Bart Tubbs, was working with the rest of the linebackers and defensive backs on some zone defenses against Tom's passing offense.

Bart Tubbs was supposed to have been one of Matt Warren's best draft-day moves two years ago. But since Tubbs had gotten to the pros, he'd been involved in a couple of fights at clubs and had been picked up once for driving without a license.

On the field, he hadn't come close to being the player he'd been in college, or the one the Bulldogs expected him to be. He'd never come close to challenging Oradell for the starting job.

All of his off-the-field trouble had been in his rookie year. But as far as Charlie was concerned, the real problem with Bart Tubbs was that he hardly ever caused any trouble for the opposing team, be it tackling, dropping back into coverage, or forcing turnovers.

"This may be just the chance that Bart needed," Joe Warren said. "And a chance to reward Matt's faith in the young man."

Charlie didn't say anything.

Mr. Warren noticed. "You don't agree?"

Charlie took a deep breath.

"You always want me to tell you the truth, right?"

"I think I've already mentioned that I've got enough people around telling me what I want to hear, Charlie."

Charlie feeling as if he were standing next to Coach Dayley during a Cardinals game. He took another deep breath and said, "Even though Oradell's hurt, Bart shouldn't start."

"You really think that?"

"I've watched him when he's played," Charlie said. "His specialty is getting in on tackles that somebody else already made. I see guys on my team, the Cardinals, like that. Making themselves look busy, but not really doing anything. And one more thing, Mr. Warren? He can't cover *you*."

On the field Bart Tubbs seemed to be in perfect position to break up a pass in the flat, but mistimed his jump, and Tom Pinkett still got a completion out of it.

Joe Warren said, "Can we get by with him and still be a solid defense the rest of the way?"

The old man was seriously picking his brain here, so Charlie knew enough to pick his *words* carefully.

"No, I don't think so," Charlie said. "I think there's going to be way too many times when it looks as if we're playing ten against eleven if he's in the middle."

It made the old man smile. "Well, doesn't that suck through a straw?"

Charlie laughed, not knowing whether it was what Mr. Warren had just said or the way he'd said it.

"It would be a lot funnier if we hadn't wasted another high draft pick on him."

"I sure didn't think it was wasted at the time," Charlie said. "Nobody did."

"If he can't help us when we need him to help us, it was wasted."

They went back to watching practice. But Charlie kept trying to sneak looks at Mr. Warren. He had been in such a good mood until they started talking about Bart Tubbs, happy about yesterday's win, happy to have Charlie as company, unless he was faking it. Mostly happy about the way the season had started.

When Bart Tubbs did break up a pass Charlie said, "Maybe

he's not as bad as I think. And the guys around him and behind him can pick him up and we still can be a solid defense."

The old man turned, pointed a finger at Charlie. Hand shaking, as usual.

"Now that right there sounded *exactly* like somebody trying to tell me what I want to hear."

Charlie knew it was true.

Twenty-Two

MR. WARREN SAID HE'D WALK Charlie to the car when practice was over.

But when they came out of the elevator, Mr. Warren said he'd forgotten to do something, mumbling to himself, saying he'd lose his head if it wasn't attached to his ancient body. He took Charlie by the arm, telling him to come on. Mr. Warren walked faster than he usually did until he was knocking on a door that said "Film Room."

When the door opened, the person on the other side of it was Tom Pinkett. He was already out of his pads, just wearing a gray Bulldogs football T-shirt and black workout shorts that came down to his knees, his hair still wet, Charlie not sure whether he'd taken the world's quickest shower once practice ended, or whether he was still sweating.

Grinning at Mr. Warren.

Charlie knowing in that moment he'd been set up.

But in a good way.

"You must be Charlie," Tom Pinkett said, sticking out his right hand.

Charlie shook his hand.

"Wow" was the best he could do.

"Boy can talk about football till the cows come," Joe Warren said. "But put him in the presence of a live player and it's as if he's lost the ability to speak."

"It's so nice to meet you," Charlie said.

"No," Tom Pinkett replied, "it's nice for *me* to finally meet *you* with something more than a text."

Charlie looked at Mr. Warren. "So we aren't going to the car?"

"Not just yet, no."

"I was about to take a closer look at Sunday's game," Tom said. "And Mr. Warren thought you might want to join me."

"If I'd played the way you did," Charlie said, "I'd want to watch that last drive until my eyes fell out of my head."

"But what I want you to watch on that drive isn't what I did right. I want you to see what I did wrong, especially on one play that could have cost us the game."

"The throw to Harrison that nearly got picked off?" Charlie said.

Tom turned to Joe Warren. "Smart boy."

"What," Mr. Warren said, "you needed more proof than how much he likes you?"

"How much time do Charlie and I have?" Tom said.

"I don't have to be anywhere," Charlie said, a little too quickly, and loudly.

"Text your mom and tell her you're going to be a little late," Joe Warren said. "If it's all right with her it's all right with me."

It was all right, his mom saying she just wanted him home by six thirty at the latest. Mr. Warren said he had some calls to make up in his office before he called it a day. He'd be back in a little while. When he was gone Tom Pinkett told Charlie he'd cleared it with his coaches for Charlie to sit with him, see the game film shot by the team's video coordinator from his perch in the press box.

The guy Tom called his "eye in the sky."

It was actually like a small theater, the cushy seats rising up toward the back of the room, Charlie starting to wonder if they were going to have buttered popcorn and soft drinks, too.

"You're going to see what the coaches see from upstairs, like the snapshots that get sent down for me to look at while the game is going on," Tom said. "And what I'm supposed to be seeing in real time."

"Cool," Charlie said.

They were in the front row. Tom hit a button on the arm of his chair and the room went dark. Pointed his remote at the huge screen in front of them. "Lights, camera, action," he said. "Isn't that what they say in the movies?"

"Something like that," Charlie said. Ridiculously, stupidly excited to be here with him, just looking at the image on the screen, Tom frozen over center.

"Before we start," he said, "I want to tell you something, just between the two of us."

Charlie Gaines and the quarterback of the L.A. Bulldogs. Sitting here being boys. Tom about to tell him something that was supposed to stay in the room, the way things were supposed to stay in the locker room.

"I was thinking about something after Sunday's game. About how the last person to change my life this way—just by believing in me the way you did—was my coach in high school. Only this time it was a twelve-year-old," Tom said. "Unbelievable."

"Thank you," Charlie said.

"No," Tom said. "Thank *you*."

Tom hit Play.

Charlie saw that it was some view from upstairs, taking in the whole field, all twenty-two players, Charlie focusing on Tom as he went into a quick three-step drop in the middle of the last drive, forcing a throw to Harrison Mays that was nearly intercepted, ball bouncing out of the defender's hands and into Harrison's to get the Bulldogs a big third-down conversion.

"You know why that happened, Charlie?" Tom said. "Because even though I had been working the other side of the field on the drive up to then, they knew that when I absolutely had to have yards, I was going back to my favorite receiver, Harrison. The corner knew it and jumped the route, and it was only dumb luck that he didn't take it the other way."

He played it again.

"See what I mean? He *knew*."

"Yeah," Charlie said. "He acted like he knew what play was coming."

Tom Pinkett nodded. "Even Peyton Manning cost the Colts a Super Bowl one time because a corner for the Saints jumped a route that way."

All day long, sitting with Mr. Warren, Charlie had felt like he was on the inside again, the way he had been the first day the two of them had watched practice on the field.

But this was different.

Better.

Tom went back, started the play again, paused the picture, got up, walked to the screen, showed Charlie how the corner was coming at full speed before Tom even released the ball.

"He knew I'd go back to what was working for me, even if I hadn't run that play since the end of the first half," he said. "And guess what? Sometimes you can get by with that." Tom Pinkett winked at Charlie now the way the old man did sometimes and said, "But sometimes you gotta throw them a curveball. Just to keep them on their toes."

Charlie smiled. Not because Tom Pinkett had made a bad throw. No, he was smiling in the small, dark theater because he was in this room with *him*, the great Tom Pinkett, someone he never thought he'd get anywhere near.

But feeling totally at home.

Twenty-Three

THE BULLDOGS FELL TO 2-2 in their next game, losing to the Eagles in Philadelphia.

Tom Pinkett threw four touchdown passes to go with two interceptions—one returned for a touchdown, maybe his worst read of the season so far—but even the four touchdowns couldn't give his team a decent chance to win on this day, thanks to a total meltdown by the defense.

The worst of it, Charlie saw—everybody watching the game saw—was the linebacker play. There just seemed to be this huge hole in the middle of the L.A. defense, one that the Eagles exploited from their first drive of the game—hammering away the running game and mixing things up with short passes that couldn't be stopped and that kept turning into large gains. Bart Tubbs, who kept trying to cover the area Troy Aikman called the "deep middle," wound up with his back to the play more often than not, chasing the ballcarrier. Never a good thing for a line-backer.

"Sometimes that deep middle for Bart looks like a deep sink-hole," Aikman said at one point.

"Actually," Anna said to Charlie, "it looks like they're asking Bart to cover the middle of the ocean. Only he can't swim."

They were watching at her house. Charlie had wondered if she'd even want to watch the game with him, the way she'd been acting cool to him since that night in the park.

But she'd called and invited him. So they watched together as the Eagles kept ringing up points, over five hundred yards in total offense, in what looked like a three-hour train wreck if you were a Bulldogs fan.

It wasn't just Bart, of course. Defense is a team game. Yet the team sure looked a lot different with Tubbs in the middle of it. And a defense that had been one of the surprises of the first quarter of the season suddenly looked more like a Pop Warner unit trying to keep up with grown men.

Anna suggested that Coach Fiore could move either Alex Beech or Chuck Stoner, one of their two outside backers, to the middle.

"Nah, they're good where they are, not that you can tell so today," Charlie said. "Besides, some famous coach said that you never weaken one position to strengthen another."

"We're in deep trouble without Oradell," Anna said.

"We just need to find somebody a lot better than Bart to play there."

Then Charlie reminded her of a guy named Chase Blackburn, who had basically been sitting on his couch when the Giants signed him late one season, what turned out to be the season they won their second Super Bowl against the Patriots.

"Remember him?" Charlie said. "We were watching the Giants play the Packers right after Thanksgiving and he made an interception and I was, like, 'Who the heck is number 93?'"

"And I said, wait, there's a player in the league you don't know?"

"I knew him," Charlie said. "I just didn't know he was back on their team. He had been cut. But from that game on, he played great for the Giants all the way through the Super Bowl. Even intercepted a Tom Brady pass that ended up being the biggest defensive play of the game."

"Yeah," Anna said. "People kept talking about the middle linebacker the Giants basically found on the street. Well, we need to find ourselves a street like that."

"Yup," Charlie said.

And just like that, he knew just the right street.

Twenty-Four

WHEN HE GOT HOME HE went straight upstairs, sat down in front of his laptop like he was working on an assignment for school. Only this felt way more important to him than school right now.

He wasn't even going to tell Anna, at least not yet, because he didn't want to be talked out of it, because he knew if he tried to explain to her about the guy he was thinking about he was going to sound like some kind of crazy person.

Because the guy he was thinking about was Jack "Sack" Sutton. The actor.

Charlie went back now and read articles on Jack Sutton he'd read before. Went to YouTube and ESPN.com and looked at old highlights, going all the way back to when Jack Sutton should have won the Heisman, when he was the best college football player in the country at the University of Miami. Back when he was constantly getting in trouble.

Then he left college early for the pros and got into even more trouble, like he didn't just want to be like Lawrence Taylor on the field—he wanted to outdo Taylor off the field. The most athletic linebacker in years, acting like life was one big party without rules. Then came that hit to his knee. And the operation. And the game was over.

"Too little, too late," Jack Sutton had said to Charlie that day on Alvarado Street.

But was it too late?

He was still only twenty-seven years old, just twenty-seven last month, Charlie looked that up, too. But Charlie knew this wasn't just about his age, or the condition of his knee, or the condition of the rest of him. Even if he wanted to play—and Charlie had no way of knowing whether he did or not—who knew if he still could after being out of it for so long?

Who knew if Mr. Warren and Matt would even want anything to do with him? That was how much trouble he'd caused for himself and the Jaguars.

There was the story about the brawl Jack started in a New York club. And about the rental car he'd totaled in New Orleans after a night of partying, though they never got to test him for drunk driving because he left the car on Poydras Street near the Superdome, went straight to the airport, and left town.

There was the six-game suspension he got at the start of his last season for picking up an assistant coach and body-slamming him to the ground after practice one day.

"I got tired of a guy who could never play football worth a lick telling me how to play football" was his explanation to the commissioner.

Then came the knee injury, and the three surgeries, and the failed comeback with the Jaguars in training camp the year before last. Finally Jack Sutton retired, moved to L.A., announced he was trying acting full time after a few well-received appearances on *Fright Night Lights*.

After an hour Charlie rubbed his eyes, closed his laptop, and thought:

This is nuts.

I am nuts.

Twenty-Five

CHARLIE DECIDED HE WOULD TELL Mr. Warren in person, at the Bulldogs' practice on Monday afternoon.

Charlie still hadn't told Anna, worried that she might clown him on the spot. It was funny, if you thought about it, he was more scared of telling her his idea than he was her grandfather, who only owned the team.

So he'd wait and see what kind of reaction he got. Good or bad, or even if Mr. Warren burst out laughing. If the idea went anywhere—meaning if Joe Warren thought it was worth placing a call to Jack Sutton or his agent—Charlie would tell Anna first thing.

On the way to the stadium Charlie and Carlos talked about how quickly the season had gone wrong after such a promising start, after the city had started feeling better about the Bulldogs than it ever had, Mr. Warren feeling the exact same way.

"This can't happen to us all over again," Carlos said.

"Lot of football left to be played," Charlie said, knowing he sounded like a coach, but meaning what he said. "We both know how long these seasons are."

"You have no idea how long they can get around here."

When they got upstairs Mr. Warren's secretary told Charlie to go right in. Mr. Warren smiled when he saw Charlie come through the door, the way he always did.

Charlie noticed he had some printouts in his hand.

"I've been looking at the names of some of the linebackers on the waiver wire," he said. "The list is not pretty, Charlie boy."

"Maybe the guy we're looking for isn't on that list," Charlie said. "Did you ever think about that?"

The old man put the paper down, motioned for Charlie to take a seat on the other side of the desk.

"That sounds mysterious. You got somebody for me? Did you find me the Tom Pinkett of NFL linebackers, another guy the league was about to forget?"

"It's going to sound way crazier than that, Mr. Warren, trust me."

"How about you tell me what's on your mind and then I'll be the one to say how crazy it is or not," Joe Warren said.

"But if you do think it is," Charlie said, "crazy, I mean, you promise you won't tell anybody that I even brought it up in the first place?"

"Not even if I get my own podcast," the old man said.

Then Charlie told him about Jack Sutton.

Told him all of it: seeing him on the movie set, seeing him run.

He told him about Chase Blackburn going back to the Giants that year and helping take them to the Super Bowl. How sometimes you found the guy you were looking for on the street, and how Anna had told Charlie the Bulldogs needed to find that street.

Talking fast, not wanting to lose his nerve.

When he finally finished, Mr. Warren didn't say anything right away.

But he didn't laugh, either.

They were sitting outside now, on the perch above the field, practice over. Mr. Warren had his feet up on the chair in front of him, wearing the same soft-looking, scuffed brown shoes he always did.

It was one of those days when he looked more tired than usual. More shake to his hand when he put his water bottle to his lips, taking what he called his "afternoon pill," which he said wasn't to be confused with his morning and evening pills.

They were still talking about Jack Sutton.

"I wanted to draft him, you know. Badly. Despite what a bad boy he was."

"I read that," Charlie said.

Mr. Warren turned and grinned. "Course you did. But then we didn't draft him, for all the reasons Matt gave me and even some he didn't. And then when he started to get into all that trouble after he got to the league, Matt said, 'Told you so, Dad.' Told me that some of those young actors and actresses in Hollywood, they have star power, too. But they blow it all in the end because they don't have any discipline. Or character. They act like their talent is a part-time job and their full-time job is going to parties."

The old man paused, waved his hand in the air in front of him, Charlie thinking it looked like a paper floating in a breeze.

"*Then* the boy got hurt and Matt said, see, it would've been a wasted pick even if we had put up with all his nonsense for a few years. It was then that I had to remind him about the fallacy of the predetermined outcome."

"The *what*?"

"Assuming that if you could have changed just one thing that happened in a game, everything else that happened afterward would have played out exactly the same way," Joe Warren said. "Guy gets caught stealing in a baseball game, next guy hits a home run, the announcers say, 'Well, that should have been a two-run homer.' Except they don't know if the next guy would have been pitched differently with a guy on second. Maybe that home run never happens."

"I see what you mean," Charlie said.

Mr. Warren said, "So maybe things go differently for Jack Sutton if he plays for us. Maybe even if he plays for somebody like me, who knows. Maybe he doesn't get hurt, maybe he would have cleaned up his act. Or maybe being in L.A. would have just meant more temptations for him and more trouble. Who's to say?"

He paused now and turned to look at Charlie. "You say you saw him run?"

Charlie nodded. "Like the wind."

Joe Warren said, "We have no idea if he even wants to try to come back."

"Nope."

"But you really believe that if he *could* get himself into football shape, and do it fast, that he could help us?"

"What I think, Mr. Warren, is that we've got nothing to lose by asking him."

We.

Meaning it as much right then as he ever had, knowing it was like he was laying his love for the team on the line by coming here, by making this suggestion.

"You only get so many chances," the old man said in a quiet voice. "Jack Sutton, before he got hurt, he probably thought he could play forever. Then he found out differently. Who knows? Maybe now that he found out that he wasn't going to have all the chances and all the seasons he wanted, he might want what they all want in sports."

"What's that?"

"One more shot," Joe Warren said. He slapped his thigh now. "You know what, Charlie? You're right about something. What's the worst thing he can say to me? No? People have been saying no to me my whole life. For years they said, no, you can't bring football back to L.A. You think about it, Charlie, my own team's been saying no to me from the start, the way all these seasons have ended."

"We need to have a better ending this time, Mr. Warren."

Joe Warren said, "Maybe a guy from the movies can help us out with that."

Charlie reminded him that Jack Sutton hadn't played middle linebacker since high school, he'd looked that up, too. But Mr. Warren said that with the way defense was played nowadays, it wouldn't be that big of an adjustment. And might even help him if he'd lost a couple of steps due to surgery.

Charlie agreed. Thinking once again there was more to this old man when it came to football than he liked to let on.

Joe Warren stood up now, not looking tired all of a sudden, not looking tired at all, slapped his thigh again, the sound louder than before.

"Never forget something, Charlie," he said. "This is L.A. And *everyone* in this town loves a good story."

Twenty-Six

IT TURNED OUT THAT JACK Sutton was still interested in playing football.

Extremely interested.

Joe Warren found out when he called Jack himself, electing not to bother with a middleman. Sutton told him that he hadn't rehabbed his knee as hard as he had because of any hope of ever playing again—he'd just wanted to be able to walk up a flight of stairs without pain when he was fifty years old.

"Being able to outrun Vin Diesel in the movies was just an added bonus," he told Mr. Warren.

Jack Sutton explained that he had found this trainer in New York City named Ming Chew who'd gotten Jason Kidd back in the playoffs one time when Kidd was supposed to be through for the season.

The guy didn't believe that surgery was the answer to every

single sports injury, believed in acupuncture and deep-tissue massage and some other treatments that went right over Charlie Gaines's head.

Jack Sutton, with nothing much to do between football and when he got serious with acting, moved to New York for three months and worked out with Ming Chew every day. And started to feel a little better, then a lot better, happy to be living a pain-free life, still thinking he had closed the book on football.

At that point in the conversation Mr. Warren said he told Jack Sutton, "Start thinking about opening that book back up, son."

Two days later, seven in the morning, Mr. Warren and Matt Warren and Coach Nick Fiore watched Jack Sutton go through his first workout since he'd retired from the Jaguars. First out of pads, then in them. Agility drills. Sprints.

The Bulldogs' quarterback coach, David Bartlett, and their receivers coach Elijah Martellus, a former tight end in the league, showed up after an hour, and they ran some plays, asking Jack Sutton to cover Elijah, short and deep.

Mr. Warren gave Charlie the full play-by-play over the phone as soon as Charlie was out of school.

"He's slower than he was, but not as slow doing football things as we expected him to be," Mr. Warren said. "One of the reasons might be he's about twenty pounds lighter than he was the day he hurt his knee, because he wanted to make himself real pretty for the camera."

"But he looked good?" Charlie said.

Still not believing this might actually happen.

"He looked good, Charlie boy."

"What did Matt think?"

He heard the old man chuckle.

"Not gonna lie, he was a little, oh, resistant at first," Joe Warren said. "That's why we held the workout at seven o'clock in the morning, so no one but those of us involved would be there. Matt said that we'd turn into laughingstocks all over again if it got out that we were now auditioning action stars, people would want to know when Arnold Schwarzenegger and Sylvester Stallone were going to get tryouts."

There was a pause at Mr. Warren's end before he continued.

"But he liked what he saw in the workout. Then he got with our coach. And our coach said that he'd sign someone from reality TV if he thought the guy could help our team. And that he thought Mr. Sutton could help our team."

"So what are we going to do?" Charlie said.

"Did."

"Huh?"

"What we *did*, about an hour ago," the old man said, "is sign Jack Sutton to a free agent deal, since it turned out the Jags had no future claim on him, never dreaming that he'd play football again. It will be announced in the morning unless some Twitterer finds out first."

"I can't believe you actually did it!" Charlie yelled into the phone.

"Believe it," Mr. Warren said. "And then cross your fingers and keep them crossed that he does have some football in him when he starts hitting people and they hit him back."

"Got 'em crossed already," Charlie said. "Both hands."

"And, Charlie?" Joe Warren said. "Let's keep this between the two of us until we announce the signing tomorrow. Let's us be in control of this story instead of chasing it, like we did with Tom Pinkett."

"Okay," Charlie said.

He knew that meant Anna would be surprised tomorrow along with anybody else when the news broke, and Charlie knew how much she hated surprises. But he wasn't about to go against her grandfather's wishes. The old man had never asked anything of Charlie until just now and he wasn't going to let him down.

"You really think Jack can still play, Mr. Warren?" Charlie said.

"What I'm doing is thinking positively, Charlie boy!" Joe Warren said, his voice suddenly coming so loud out of the phone Charlie thought he'd accidentally put him on speaker. "We both have to tell ourselves that this is going to work out for all of us."

Deal, Charlie thought. He'd think positively enough for the entire city of Los Angeles.

Twenty-Seven

CHARLIE DIDN'T ATTEND JACK SUTTON'S press conference. He even asked Mr. Warren to keep him out of the story if there was any way for him to do that.

The old man said, no, they weren't going to start trying to hide things now.

So what he told everybody when he introduced Jack Sutton as the newest Bulldog was that his friend Charlie Gaines's mom worked in the movie business, that Charlie had seen Jack running in the new Vin Diesel movie, Charlie had mentioned it to him, and the Warrens had taken it from there.

Jack Sutton said, "I've been accused of acting like a twelve-year-old plenty of times in my football career, but I've never had to publically thank one until now."

Jack told everybody that he hadn't learned anything that he

didn't already know about football while he'd been retired, but he had learned a lot about himself, and how much the game meant to him.

And how much he'd missed it during his time away.

"I can't go back and undo the things I did when I was younger," he said. "And I know that everybody here is going to wait and see if I back up what I'm telling you today. But what I'm telling you is that I'm a different guy off the field, even if I plan to show the Warrens and Coach Fiore and Bulldog fans that I'm the same player I always was when I'm on it."

He smiled then.

"I know a lot of the people in this room mostly remember me for being an idiot," he said. "I plan to show all of you that I got a whole lot smarter once I thought football was taken away from me for good."

When Joe and Matt Warren stepped to the microphone together, Matt Warren said that this was a do-over for the Bulldogs, like they were finally drafting Jack "Sack" Sutton the second time around.

One of the local reporters asked if this was another example of the Bulldogs taking advice from their seventh-grade assistant.

Matt shook it off. "Then you better go tell our coach that he's the one with a seventh-grade assistant, because once we worked Jack out, he was more enthusiastic than anybody about us signing him."

The media had some fun with the whole thing for a couple of days, Charlie's role in the signing a big part of the story, one guy on KABC saying that this was like the kids' version of *Moneyball*, Dan Patrick calling it "Charlieball" on his radio show. So Charlie was back in the spotlight again. People more willing to give him the benefit of the doubt this time around, willing to believe that if his advice worked with Tom Pinkett, maybe it would work with Jack Sutton.

Bill Spencer wrote in the *Times* that if anybody else in the movie business spotted any possible prospects, by all means to call Joe Warren as soon as possible.

As for Anna? All she said the next day was "Wow, Gaines, now you can keep a secret almost as well as you can play fantasy football." She left it at that, which Charlie took as good. If there had been a football around, he would have happily spiked it.

Jack Sutton's first game, first since he'd unretired, was against his old team, the Jaguars, at Bulldogs Stadium. It could not have gone better if Charlie had been writing the game story himself before the game was even played. Sack Sutton lived up to his nickname right away, getting his first sack in more than two years, recovering a fumble, in there for about three-quarters of the Bulldogs' snaps on defense. Somehow played, as just about everybody said or wrote afterward, as if he'd never been hurt and never been away and—oh, by the way?—had played middle linebacker his whole career.

"A Hollywood ending for a guy who'd retired to Hollywood," Al Michaels said on *Football Night in America*. "Now everybody can't wait until next week to see what he's got planned for a sequel."

"Forget about a sequel," Cris Collinsworth said. "This might turn out to be a series for the L.A. Bulldogs."

The Bulldogs were 3–2, everybody officially treating them like the surprise team of the NFL season so far, Charlie not believing how well things were going.

Until things started to go wrong.

A little bit at first. Then a lot.

Against the Seahawks, Jack covered the wrong guy when he was supposed to be covering the tight end. The guy was wide open, and the Seahawks got handed a gift score that cost the Bulldogs a game they ended up losing by a point. A tough loss against a divisional foe vying to make the playoffs.

The week after was worse: a penalty for a late hit, at home, one the whole sport ended up talking about, just because nobody could believe what they'd seen from a guy who had cleaned up his act so perfectly.

The Bulldogs looked to have their game against the Rams won. With under ten seconds left, the Rams' quarterback was trying to get out of bounds at midfield, hoping to get one more play for his team, one Hail Mary heave into the end zone. Bulldogs about to clinch the win, leading 17–15.

Jack Sutton chasing the QB.

Maybe wanting to end the game right there by causing a fumble. Problem was, this was the Jack Sutton who was a couple of steps slower than he'd been in his prime, even with the occasional flashes of his old brilliance he'd shown so far in his comeback.

That Jack Sutton trying to catch up to the play.

The runner beating Jack to the sideline. By a lot. One foot deep into that fat white stripe that means you've made it out of bounds. And either Jack couldn't stop himself, or just didn't see that the guy had made it out of bounds.

But what everybody in the stadium, and everybody watching on television, saw was Sack Sutton shoving a helpless QB with both hands, knocking him into one of his assistant coaches.

The Rams players standing there went crazy, flags flew, the stadium suddenly got as quiet, Charlie thought, as the school library.

Fifteen-yard penalty, personal foul.

Ball went from the fifty to the Bulldogs' thirty-five. From there the Rams' kicker nailed a fifty-two yard field goal as time expired.

St. Louis 18, Los Angeles 17.

Not just a bad loss, but a bad division loss, as bad as you could possibly have.

Charlie was at the game, sitting where he always sat, with Mr. Warren and Anna. Mr. Warren didn't say anything when the game was over, nobody in the suite said anything.

Or moved.

It felt to Charlie as if it took Matt Warren about fifteen seconds to get from his suite next door to his father's, Charlie seeing him before anybody else did, seeing how fast he was moving, worried that Matt Warren was about to get flagged for a personal foul, just because of the look on his face.

Matt Warren stood in front of them, Charlie and Anna and his father, arms crossed, face red. He looked at his father first, then shot a quick look at Charlie.

Then back to Joe Warren.

"I should have known better," he said, spitting out his words. "I knew it, I knew it, I *knew* it. But I went along one more time."

His dad didn't say anything. Charlie wasn't even breathing.

"The great Sack Sutton," Matt Warren said. "At least when he was totaling cars and busting up clubs, the only person he was hurting was himself."

That was it, all he had. He turned and walked out, almost bumping into the only other person in the suite who was moving in that moment, one of the waitresses.

Charlie feeling in that moment as if the real loser at Bulldogs Stadium was himself.

Just like that the twelve-year-old who had encouraged the owner to sign Tom Pinkett and then Jack Sutton wasn't the most adorable football boy in town anymore.

The headline the next day over Bill Spencer's column in the *Times* read this way:

BOY AND HIS DOGS SACKED FOR LOSS

The next night even Mr. Fallon took some rips at Charlie and the old man on his radio show. After he tried to soften the blows by telling his listeners how much he loved Charlie, reminded them that he coached Charlie on his son's Pop Warner football team, reminded him that he was the one who started letting Charlie give his fantasy picks on the show.

"With all due respect, I've never met a kid who loves football more, or tries harder on the field," Steve Fallon said.

Charlie braced himself, just knowing that whatever came next wasn't going to be good, because it was like his mom had always told him, nothing good ever came after "all due respect."

"But my job," Steve Fallon continued, "is to give my opinions about the big issues in the world of L.A. sports. And unfortunately, Joe Warren has made Charlie Gaines, as great a kid as he is, into an issue. The two of them decided to bring in Jack Sutton, and now Sutton might end up costing the Bulldogs the first playoff spot in the team's history. The truth is, the kid's latest fantasy pick has turned into a total nightmare."

When the show ended a minute later, Charlie immediately got a text message from Anna.

How do u like being a member of the family so far?

Twenty-Eight

THE WEIRD THING WAS, CHARLIE was still killing it in his fantasy leagues the way he always had, solidly in first place in every league except for one head-to-head league, stuck behind a kid he knew only as the owner of a team called Dream Team. He was one of those guys who loved trash-talking Charlie online even though Charlie refused to respond. You got guys like that from time to time, and this kid would send the same message each week:

"You will never beat me."

Whatever. Charlie was beating everybody else. He had never thought there was any magic to the whole thing, just common sense. Charlie knew how fantasy football had changed as the NFL had become more and more of a passing league, knew that all the changes to protect the quarterback and to put more passing offense and scoring into the game had changed the landscape of fantasy football forever.

Teams were throwing the ball more and quarterbacks were putting up greater fantasy point totals week by week, year by year. Charlie loved going back into pro football's past to measure just how much things *had* changed, not just to see it with his own eyes, but with his own numbers. For example: In 2002, Brett Favre was one of the great quarterbacks of his time in the NFL. He attempted 551 passes that year, which was good for fifth-most in the league. But when you looked at the league ten years later, that was the same number Sam Bradford of the Rams attempted in 2012, which only placed him *eleventh* in the NFL.

It wasn't just pass attempts. Before 2011, Charlie knew, a quarterback had only thrown for five thousand yards *twice* in league history. But then *three* guys did it in 2011 alone—Drew Brees, Tom Brady, and Matthew Stafford—and Brees did it again in 2012.

In 2003 Peyton Manning led the NFL with 4,267 passing yards. Nine years later that would have only been good for ninth-best in the league.

In Charlie's world, the numbers never lied, or let him down. In 2013 five quarterbacks threw more than thirty touchdown passes. Back in 2002, though, only one quarterback did it and only one did it a year later. And over the same decade the number of thousand-yard rushers had gone down as the passing stats just kept piling up.

The first couple of rounds of a fantasy draft used to be reserved for the league's top running backs. No more. Touchdown passes had increased in value from four to six points, and wide receivers were getting a point per reception. So now more and more quarterbacks and receivers were going earlier and earlier in drafts, which was really just common sense, and simple math. The days when you could make what you thought was a safe early-round pick for a running back were gone, gone, gone.

That wasn't just math to Charlie, it was science, and hardly rocket science, not if you worked at it the way he did. And one thing Charlie knew was that nobody was ever going to outwork him or outresearch him.

Another thing paying off for Charlie, the way it usually did: He had waited until his later rounds to go for defense, because no matter how much studying and homework you did, it was still difficult to predict—starting with the injury factor—who the dominant defenses were going to be from year to year. ESPN.com had the New York Jets ranked thirty-two out of thirty-two teams in the preseason, and halfway through the season the Jets had a winning record due mainly to their defense.

In fantasy leagues, you got defensive points based on how many points your defense gave up. If your team gave up zero to seven points, you got ten points; seven to thirteen, you got eight. Then you added in the points not just for tackles but for sacks, interceptions, and defensive touchdowns. The number of tackles was obviously huge for your defense, which is why if you had a star like Luke Kuechly of the Panthers making a lot of tackles week to week, your defense became a consistent point-getter for you, made you feel like you had a star quarterback on your defense the way you needed one on offense.

And Charlie looked at more than stats when evaluating his own defensive guys; he looked at schedules, too. Which teams had the weakest ones. Which teams were going to be going up against rookie quarterbacks.

It was all working for him again, working in all his leagues. There was his "keeper" league, where you could keep players from the previous year. Charlie was also in a rotisserie-style league, where your ranking wasn't determined by your won-loss record, but rather by an overall average of your team's statistics.

Rotisserie leagues, he knew, probably were a better indicator of who truly had the best team over a regular season, then into the playoffs. But for the sheer fun and competition, Charlie loved going head-to-head. Feeling like he had a big game every single week. Charlie just flat-out liked head-to-head leagues the best, the challenge each year of looking for the best defense exactly the way you looked for the quarterback who could light it up for you.

Then once the season started it was your quarterback, two running backs, two wide receivers, tight end, kicker, and defense against somebody else every week, straight up, the final score usually looking like a big NBA score, 120–110 or something like that if you won.

If you tried to explain it to non-fantasy guys you would see their eyes start to glaze over, like you were trying to hypnotize them or put them to sleep. He'd tried with his mom, just once, over dinner, and she'd finally told him she'd double his allowance if he'd stop.

Oh, he had his swings and misses, sometimes big ones, everybody did. But he was still the guy the other kids at Culver City Middle came to for help. In that world—his old world—he was still the king.

Just not the real world.

Charlie had found out—the hard way—that picking the wrong guy or the wrong guys in fantasy didn't hurt the way it did when the games counted, when it was the NFL and mistakes really could cost your season. More than ever, he understood just how much pressure Matt Warren really was under, every draft, every year, every personnel decision.

Every single time he was on the line making a pick.

Things only got worse for the Bulldogs in their rematch the following week against the 49ers. Tom Pinkett had an up-and-down day, throwing three touchdown passes and two interceptions. And the Dogs' rookie kick returner, Isaiah Browne, fumbled one punt after a twenty-yard return, and then just flat missed another—with both leading to San Francisco scores. The Bulldogs lost, 41–28, their third loss in a row.

Jack Sutton's game was more down than up. He had a couple more costly penalties—a defensive holding call that gave the 49ers a key first down, and then a hit to the helmet penalty that ruined what would have been an interception.

He did show flashes of the old Sack Sutton talent, though. There was one play when he blew past two blockers as the 49ers'

QB was trying to run an option, swung his arm and knocked the ball loose, giving the Bulldogs a turnover that Tom Pinkett took advantage of by driving the offense right down the field for a touchdown that, for the moment at least, gave everyone hope.

It was like Jack was teasing Bulldogs fans, showing them just enough to keep him in there, showing he still had big plays and big moments in him.

But Charlie—Charlie the numbers guy—knew that Jack was still giving too many big plays to the other team.

Charlie was with Anna the day after the 49ers game, the Bulldogs having hardly any turnaround time because they had the Thursday night game against the Browns at Bulldogs Stadium. As usual, Mr. Warren had invited Charlie to sit in the suite even though Charlie wouldn't have blamed him if he didn't want him around, at practice or at games, the way things were going.

Charlie had told his mom he might not want to go; the last thing Mr. Warren needed was to be seen sitting next to him on national television, something that would give the Thursday night announcers a chance to make fun of both of them.

"You should go," his mom had said before Anna came over. "If Joe Warren didn't want you there, he wouldn't have invited you."

"So you're, like, ordering me to go to a football game on a school night?"

"Pretty much," she'd said, and kissed him on top of his head. "Go figure."

"Why couldn't I have kept my stupid opinions to myself?" Charlie'd said.

"They weren't stupid just because they aren't working out right now," she'd said. "And anyway, that's not the way you roll." She'd given her head a quick shake then, like getting cobwebs out, and said, "Did I just say that? The way you *roll*?"

Charlie had just replayed the conversation for Anna, finishing by saying, "My mom's hardly ever wrong on the big stuff. But I *should* have kept my big fat mouth shut."

And that's when Anna said, "You should have."

Sitting cross-legged on Charlie's rug, leaning back against his bed, laptop and microphone and power cord between them, a plate of cookies next to her, having just finished *The Charlie Show*.

Charlie said, "Not exactly the answer I was looking for."

"Then maybe this is another time when you should have kept your mouth shut."

She added: "I mean, you did a pretty good job of that when you didn't tell me about Jack Sutton."

"Wait a second," Charlie said. "You acted like you were cool with it when it happened. You hardly said anything about it at all."

"There's no law that I have to tell you everything I'm thinking," she said.

"So you're saying you weren't cool with it?"

"Wasn't cool with it then, not cool with it now," she said. "You and your little secrets with Gramps."

"He asked me not to tell anybody for one day," Charlie said.

"I'm not anybody," she said.

"I just figured that if he wanted you to know, he would have told you himself."

"Knowing him as long as you have, you mean?"

"Now you're just being sarcastic."

"Gee, you *think*?"

"Great, more sarcasm."

"Deal with it."

Charlie couldn't explain it, he just felt like they were in a car now that was starting to go faster and faster, no way to put on the brakes.

"What are we really talking about here?"

"Okay, this time I'll tell you exactly what I'm thinking," Anna said. "And what I'm thinking is that we're supposed to be a team. You and me. I told you that after your big press conference with Tom Pinkett. Only we weren't a team with Jack Sutton. You know how people are always joking that there's no *i* in team? Guess I found out that there sure is one in Charlie."

"Sounds like you've been holding a lot in," Charlie said.

Anna said, "It's like something I almost told you in the park that night, but didn't. And you want to know why I didn't? Because I could see that *you* couldn't see how you were starting to get a big head. That your ego was getting in the way."

"You said nothing was bothering you."

"You really are dense, aren't you? That was the night you told me how you crushed it with the reporters."

Putting air quotes around "crushed."

Before he could respond she said, "Maybe I'm just sick of how much you've changed."

"I haven't changed."

"Really?"

"You know what this sounds like to me?" Charlie said. "Like you're piling on along with everybody else right now."

"How am I piling on when all I'm basically doing is agreeing with you? You say that you should have kept your mouth shut about Jack Sutton and I agreed. It's just that your ego doesn't like hearing the truth."

"My ego again," he said. "You make it sound like it's to blame for everything except smog."

"Nah," she said, "my biggest problem isn't your new supersized ego. It's that I liked the old Charlie better."

"I told you, I haven't changed," he said.

"Yes," she said, "you have. You started liking the attention you got from Tom Pinkett so much that you had to get that feeling again with Jack Sutton."

"That's not fair," he said.

"Isn't it?"

"No, it's not. You know me better than that."

"You know what I know? How soon you forgot that you never would have told Gramps about Tom Pinkett if I didn't make you. If I wasn't behind you the way I always am. But once it *was* out there, you started to like people treating you like a star."

"But I do seem to remember it was your idea to make me a star with our podcast."

Anna ignored that one.

She said, "This time you were going to go one better with

Gramps than you did with Tom Pinkett, sitting there on the bench in Cincinnati. This time you found a guy . . . in the movies!"

Charlie felt himself getting hot now, knowing it was a terrible idea with her, knowing getting mad at Anna never ever worked, even when they were just having one of their normal debates about almost anything, ice cream or music. Or football.

But right now he didn't care.

"You're the one who should have a talk show," Charlie said. "You seem to know everything about everything."

"I'm just telling you what I think."

"I did what I did because I love the team," Charlie said.

Standing up now.

Anna stood up, too.

"You ever think about loving it a little less sometimes?"

"You ever think about shutting up?" he said.

"Excuse me?"

"You ever think that you're not always smarter than everybody else?" Charlie said.

Feeling like the car wasn't just going too fast now, feeling as if it was out of control. And there was nothing he could do to stop it.

"Excuse me?" she said, her voice as low as he knew his was loud.

"You think you're the only one keeping things in?" Charlie said. "You think I never do? You think I don't get sick of you being such a know-it-all? Oh, I forgot, that's perfectly all right, you're always telling me you're doing it because you care about me so much. How about this? How about *you* care about me a little less?"

Now her voice was so low Charlie could barely hear it. Not that he wanted to in that moment.

"I'm sorry," Anna said, "for being your friend."

And walked out of his room, down the stairs, Charlie hearing her on the phone, asking her mother to come pick her up now.

Then he heard the front door close.

When he heard the car about ten minutes later, he went to his window, watched her get into the backseat.

She turned and looked up at him, as if she knew he was watching.

He didn't feel like Brain then. He just felt like a dope.

Twenty-Nine

MR. WARREN CALLED DURING DINNER the next night and asked if Charlie wanted to come to practice the next day. Charlie thanked him but said, no, he had some studying to do.

He wasn't lying, Charlie hated lying and liars, he did have a test on Thursday, but he could have done a total grind after school and got his studying in then.

"No problem," Mr. Warren said. "Glad to see my friend Charlie studying something besides Xs and Os. But I'll see you Thursday night for the game, right?"

Charlie covered the receiver, took a deep breath, let it out, thinking, *Okay, here goes.*

"Actually I can't do that, either, Mr. Warren. My other team, the Cardinals, has a practice that doesn't end until six at the earliest, and the Bulldogs game starts at five-thirty. I'll just have to record it and watch it from the start without knowing the score when I get home."

"I could send Carlos and you could catch the second half if you want. He won't mind missing a little of the game."

"I wouldn't want him to do that," Charlie said. "You know how much I love sitting next to you at games. I'll catch the next one, okay?"

Charlie had forgotten he had Cardinals practice when his mom had told him he should go to the game, the schedule changing from week to week depending on Coach Dayley's schedule at work. But he knew that if everything hadn't turned into this kind of crapfest—with the team, with Anna, even with the media—he might have taken Mr. Warren up on his offer.

But practice gave him an out, so he didn't have to lie to Mr. Warren and his mom. And he was going to grab it, just tell himself that this was the way things used to be before he was going to every single Bulldogs home game and sitting with the owner of the team, tell himself that when things were a lot more normal in his life, he would have been focusing as much on the Cardinals game against Palos Verdes on Saturday as he was on Bulldogs vs. Browns on Thursday night.

Only there was a new normal now for Charlie Gaines, which meant hardly anything was the way it used to be.

Oh, he'd watch the Thursday night game all right, root as hard as he ever did for the Bulldogs; as badly as things were going for them right now, they were still his team. He'd rooted for them in all the other bad times, in all the other seasons.

When he really thought about it, maybe one thing was back to the way it used to be:

He was fine with watching a Bulldogs game alone.

The Bulldogs lost again, lost even though the Browns turned the ball over four times. Tom Pinkett threw two bad picks in the fourth quarter, one on the eleven-yard line when a field goal would have tied the game and a touchdown would have put the Bulldogs ahead.

Jack Sutton played maybe half the snaps on defense, sharing time with Bart Tubbs. Each made a play that hurt the Bulldogs in the second half, Jack running right past the Browns' fullback on a screen when it looked as if he had the guy lined up for an eight-yard loss. The fullback ended up running thirty yards, down to the two-yard line.

On the NFL Network's broadcast, Mike Mayock, the analyst, said, "Maybe the next time the Bulldogs sign a free agent out of the movies, they should try for one of the Avengers."

Charlie, who usually liked Mayock, said, "And maybe your network should go get Phil Simms."

But even when Jack Sutton would make a bad play, and he was making his share, he would come back later and make a good one. Remind you of the player he used to be. And give you hope that he could figure things out before the season was over.

In the *Los Angeles Times* the next day, Charlie reading it on his phone on the way to school, Bill Spencer wrote this about Jack Sutton:

One of these days we are going to find out if a B-list actor can still be an A-lister on the football field for an entire game. There's a reason why he lights up talk shows the way he does, and you saw it again last night against the Texans: The guy continues to carry around a world of hurt with him, he just keeps directing it at the Bulldogs as much as their opponents. Like Sack Sutton is as good right now sacking himself as the other team's quarterback.

He and Anna sat together at lunch that day, as awkward as it was for both of them, everything more awkward between them than he could ever remember, and Charlie knew they both knew it. But it was also as if they both knew it would have been even more weird for them to stop having lunch together, or to avoid each other altogether, though they probably both wanted to right now. Anything would be better than ever having the kind of rock-fight of an argument they'd had.

He asked her what it had been like in the suite in the second half.

"Oh, it was tons of fun," she said.

"How was your grandfather?"

"Quiet," she said, all the traces of sarcasm gone. "The look on his face, I've seen that look before, in all the other seasons when we turned into a bunch of losers."

"They're not losers," he said. "It's a weak division. They're still only two games out of first."

"Right," she said.

"They can just as easily win some games in a row the way they've lost some."

"You really believe that?"

"What else am I gonna believe at this point?" he said. "What choice do I have? It isn't the way I'd bet, or even make with one of my fantasy picks. But I'm not betting. Or making a fantasy pick. I'm rooting."

"At least you're honest," she said. "You still crushing it in all your fantasy leagues, by the way?"

Trying to sound interested. Or just get the subject away from the Bulldogs.

"All but one."

"Still behind in that one? Must kill you, being in second in even one of them. Who's that guy tormenting you?"

"He calls himself Dream Team," Charlie said. "Don't worry. I'll pass him before the season is over."

She nodded. "There's the old ego."

Sticking the needle in, almost by force of habit.

"Let's not go there," he said. "Please?"

"Whatever."

"I'm sorry," he said. "The stuff I said."

"Good," she said, and left it there, Charlie hoping that was her way of accepting his apology, but not sure that she had. His mom talked sometimes about how there were bells you couldn't un-ring. Maybe him calling her a know-it-all was one of them.

■■■

It was Saturday morning, Culver City Cardinals against the Palos Verdes Vikings, Charlie thinking that there was at least a chance to salvage something out of his football weekend, one that had started as badly as it did with the Thursday night game. The Cardinals and Vikings were tied for first place, so today's game felt a little bit like the start of the playoffs.

Coach Dayley had actually been playing Charlie a little more the last couple of games, Charlie surprising himself by holding his own with the first stringers on defense, feeling more and more as if he belonged. Sometimes thinking he was doing a lot better defending his turf at linebacker than his man Jack Sutton was with the Bulldogs, Charlie starting to wonder if Sutton would even make it to the end of the season, worried that Matt Warren might cut him any day now.

Charlie's teammates were pretty much leaving him alone on what was happening with the Bulldogs—what Charlie had helped *make* happen—with the exception of Sean Barkley. Of course.

"Hey, Charlie!" he said when they were stretching. "Hey, Charlie Gaines! Just promise me you aren't gonna make no suggestions on improving my Lakers this season, okay?"

Charlie just laughed along with his teammates, knowing that if he came back at Sean, he'd just encourage him to keep going. All he said when the laughter stopped was "I promise, Sean, as long as you promise to kill it today against the Vikings."

They were next to each other in the grass. Charlie reached over and gave Sean some fist to pound, the subject back to football, them having a game like this to play in a few minutes, one that meant something. Coach Dayley always told them to appreciate mornings like this, they didn't know how many of them they were going to get in their lives.

It really was a perfect day for a game, and Charlie's mom was in the stands along with most of the other parents. Big-game Saturday in Culver City, for both teams, you could feel it in the air. It was all you needed in sports, whether it was Pop Warner or high school or college or the pros.

Two teams wanting the same thing.

You couldn't ask for more than that. Charlie knew *he* couldn't, not with the way things felt like they were spinning out of control lately. At least he'd have some control today, however many plays he got.

Maybe that was why the game felt even more important to him than it normally would have. There was a moment, right before the kickoff, when he looked into the stands, trying to locate his mom, eyes searching until he found her in the top row of the bleachers next to Jarrod Benedict's dad. Pretending, just for that moment, that Jarrod Benedict's smiling dad was his own.

Then he let it go, the way he always had to let it go. One more truth in his life that he couldn't run from. So he just waved at his mom, telling himself to be happy with what he had today: her, the game, first place on the line.

First place on the line.

He turned around one last time. That's when he saw the old man sitting in the far corner of the bleachers.

Thirty

THE STANDS WERE COMPLETELY empty, except for Joe Warren, by the time Charlie got to the Palos Verdes side of Memorial. Nobody ever wanted to stay around long when you lost, especially if you were the visiting team.

Mr. Warren was still in his seat, top row, corner. When Charlie got close he saw the old man was wearing a heavy Bulldogs windbreaker with leather sleeves. What was called a "throwback" jacket on their website and in the team store at the stadium, even though there was no "throwback" era for the Bulldogs because they hadn't been around long enough.

It just looked like the kind of throwback jacket you could get from the Giants and Bears and Packers and Steelers—teams that actually had a history.

"You came," Charlie said when he'd made his way to the top of the aluminum bleachers, even his rubber spikes making a lot of noise on the way up.

"Told you I'd show up one of these Saturdays," Joe Warren said, pulling down his sunglasses and giving him a wink.

Then he had both hands inside the side pockets of the jacket again like he was cold, even though this was one of those perfect L.A. mornings, Charlie's mom always telling him that L.A. was the world capital of mornings like this.

"Well," Charlie said, sitting down next to him, "at least you saw a good game."

"You were in on a couple of tackles when you were in there," Joe Warren said. "First guy in on one of them, that sweep near the end of the first half."

By now he knew the old man didn't miss very much in the game he was watching.

"You're the one always telling me that even a blind squirrel finds the acorn once in a while," Charlie said.

"I think in the modern world you might be obligated to say the nearsighted squirrel, now that I think of it," the old man said.

He smiled now at Charlie, pointed a trembling finger across the field.

"Aren't you holding up your mom?"

"I told her I was coming over to see you. She's still over there hanging with the other moms." There was just a slight pause before he added, "And dads."

"What did you tell your coach just before the fourth quarter?" Joe Warren asked. "That the other quarterback was going back to that side of the field on the interception? It was, wasn't it?"

"I just thought I saw something," Charlie said.

"You *thought* you saw something."

"Actually, Mr. Warren, I remembered something Tom Pinkett told me the day we were watching film together."

Charlie told him about what Tom had said when he walked up to the screen, how the defensive back knew what Tom was going to do.

"So you trusted that the other team's quarterback would go back to his favorite receiver with the game on the line," Joe Warren said.

"I did," Charlie said. "Tom said veteran QBs don't do it all the time. But I figured that didn't apply to a kid my age. I figured he'd trust his go-to guy."

"Wonderful thing, that kind of trust," the old man said, staring out at all the green in front of him, hunching his shoulders a little, like he wasn't just wearing his throwback jacket, but using it like a blanket.

"Bit like faith, the whole trust thing," Joe Warren said. "Sometimes you gotta believe in what you can't see. Or haven't seen yet. Might not ever see."

Sometimes, Charlie knew, you just had to let Joe Warren go. Eventually he'd get to his point. You just never knew how long it would take him. And sometimes half the fun was listening to him get there.

"Don't you stop trusting yourself because we're not seeing the results we want right now," the old man said. "Don't you stop. I haven't."

Charlie looked across the field at his friends, some still on the field, some hanging around in front of the Cardinals' bench, like they were fine with the game being over but not this best part of their day, Charlie wondering if any of them even noticed him over here. Or had any idea who the old man with him was.

Mr. Fallon would have known, but he wasn't with the Cardinals today. He was at the radio station, hosting pregame and halftime and postgame shows for the UCLA-Washington game.

"Jack Sutton was a terrible idea," Charlie said. "I wish my mom hadn't even taken me to see them shoot the movie that day. We would've all been better off."

"He did a dumb thing with that penalty, no question," Joe Warren said. "Cost us that game all by himself. But I'm not giving up on him any more than I'm giving up on you. He still shows flashes of the player he once was." He turned now, and faced Charlie. Then he smiled and said, "It's why I've decided not to cut either one of you."

"Bet Matt wants you to cut us both," Charlie said.

"No, sir, he does not."

"You've got to be kidding, Mr. Warren."

"Well, even though I *am* quite a kidder, Charlie, I'm not pulling your leg on this, mad as he was that day after the out-of-bounds penalty. My son looks at the same game film our coaches do. And what he tells me is, Sack Sutton is starting to get his groove back."

"Too late," Charlie said.

"Well, if one of us is going to worry about it getting late, it's me," Joe Warren said. "Only I'm not. Anytime I start to feel a little too old and a little too sick, you know what keeps me going, Charlie?"

Charlie didn't answer him right away. The old man had never put that word into play before.

Sick.

"Do you, Charlie?" Joe Warren said.

"No, I don't."

"I remind myself how much I love these games, how young they make me feel while they're happening, how I can't wait for the next one soon as the one we just played is over."

"Even when we lose?"

"Even then."

"And you still think we've got a legitimate shot at the playoffs?"

"It's what keeps me going," the old man said.

The two of them sat there, quiet now. There were two little kids, Jarrod Benedict's twin brothers, on the field, one of them with the ball, the other chasing.

Finally Charlie asked Joe Warren if he and Carlos could give him a ride home. The old man said absolutely they could. Charlie went back down the bleachers, helmet in his hand, ran across the field, asked his mom if that was okay with her. She said fine with her, she'd go over to Santa Monica, do some shopping and see him at home.

"It's a good thing," she said, nodding across the field.

"What?"

"Him," she said. "Being here. For you."

He ran to the car, left his jersey and helmet and pads in there, took off his football pants and put on a pair of jeans and sneakers that his mom had brought with her and a Clippers T-shirt. Sprinted back across the field and back to the top row, out of breath as he said, "You never said anything about being sick before, Mr. Warren. Are you? Sick, I mean?"

"As a matter of fact, Charlie boy, I am."

He stood up. It took some time, and some effort. Then he told Charlie to put out his arm so he could grab it like a railing, that railings were an old person's best friend, even if they were attached to a young friend of his.

Put a death grip on Charlie's forearm. The two of them made their way slowly down through the bleachers.

"Take a walk?" Joe Warren said.

"Whatever you want," Charlie said. "I have no place I need to be except with you."

"Got another true story for you," the old man said. "This one about me."

Thirty-One

THE TWO OF THEM WALKED—SLOWLY—AROUND the field at Memorial.

Every so often, without warning, the old man would stop, put his head back, let the sun hit him full in the face. Almost like he was taking a drink of it.

Then they would start up again.

"You know how our defense has been the past month, Charlie?" he was saying now. "That's what you start to feel like when you're as old as I am."

"You don't act old," Charlie said. "You don't think old. The way I look at it, that means you *aren't* old."

"But I am," Joe Warren said. "And when you are, you feel like no matter what you do, you never have enough defense to stop it. Age, I mean. It's like a game you know you can't win, no matter how hard you try."

They had made their way to the end zone, walking in front of the goalposts.

"You can try to come up with the best game plan," Joe Warren continued. "Diet and exercise and getting the proper rest and drinking so much water you feel like you've got an ocean inside you. Taking all the damn pills they want you to take. But no matter how much you do, you still know that eventually you're going get hit and go down and stay down."

"That better be some hit, Mr. Warren, to put you down."

He put a hand on Charlie's shoulder then, Charlie not sure if he was trying to steady himself, or just make a point.

"That brings me to what you asked me right before we started our walk," the old man said. "About being sick."

"Okay," Charlie said.

"You ever hear of a guy named Hodgkin, Charlie?"

Charlie said he hadn't, and the old man laughed.

"'Course you haven't," he said. "Because this Hodgkin guy never played football. They did, however, name a disease after him. Hodgkin's disease. They've even got one that they call non-Hodgkin's, though I've often thought they should have given that one to some other fella. Anyway, Charlie, that's what I'm sick with. The fancy name is non-Hodgkin's lymphoma. I didn't think I should keep it from a friend like you any longer."

He didn't break stride, kept his slow normal pace as he added, "It's a form of cancer, Charlie."

Charlie swallowed.

"Oh," he said.

Looked over at Joe Warren, talking about cancer in the same way he'd been talking about the Cardinals beating Palos Verdes.

"Oh," he said again, not knowing what else to say.

"I tell you all the time about telling the truth," Joe Warren said. "So this is my big truth, Charlie. And stop looking like you're afraid I might go down and stay down before we make it to the other end of the field. Because my doctors—and I've got enough to fill out an NFL roster, *with* practice squad—tell me that if I'm lucky, I will live out my days with this Hodgkin's. Even if it does give me some bad days from time to time."

He pointed at Charlie, no shake to his hand now, and said, "*This* day not being one of them."

They were passing the Cardinals' bench, all of the players and parents and coaches gone, the whole area cleaned up after snack, because the last person to police the area was always Coach Dayley. Like it was a crime scene.

Charlie knew everybody called him Brain. But he didn't think he was smart enough—or old enough himself—to know what he was supposed to say, how he was supposed to be responding to the news Mr. Warren had just given him.

He did come up with a question.

"Does Anna know?"

"She does," the old man said. "And has been as good at keeping it a secret from you as you were keeping the secret from her about Sack Sutton."

"She didn't like that very much."

"I heard," Joe Warren said. "Oh, did I ever hear."

"Her secret about you was bigger," Charlie said.

"But I trusted her, the way I trust you."

Then he said, "How about we sit and rest for just a minute?"

He sat down on the Cardinals' bench and Charlie sat next to him. The old man leaned back and took in more sun.

"Isn't this just the best day?" he said.

Charlie wasn't so sure about that, having heard what he'd just heard, but said, "Yes."

"Do you think we should go for ice cream after this? I think we should skip lunch and go straight to ice cream."

Charlie grinned. "Only if you keep one more secret, from my mom."

The old man put out his hand. Charlie shook it. It felt cold on a warm day.

"All my days are great ones now, Charlie, maybe because I am a little sick," the old man said. "Everybody always fusses over me when we lose a game, like if we don't start winning all the losing might kill me. And they don't understand that win or lose, I am having myself a wonderful time."

"For real?"

"We were talking about trust before? Well, I trust this team, Charlie, whether it's in a slump right now or not. I love that your friend Tom Pinkett gives us a chance to win every single game. That's never happened before with the Bulldogs, not like this."

He offered his fist to Charlie, grinning as he did. Charlie bumped him some.

"And I loved making the play for Sack Sutton, rolling the dice that way and shocking the world. And even when he screws up, I love how much he loves being back in football. Did you see when he caused that fumble at the end of the Houston game? He was jumping around on the sidelines like a little kid."

"He knew he'd screwed up earlier," Charlie said. "You could just see how much he wanted to make up for it, even if it was too late in that game."

"He's not where he's going to be, I believe that," Joe Warren said. Grinned and said, "He's better than what we had, but not as good as we'd hoped. Does that make sense?"

"Perfect sense," Charlie said.

"Two bad plays, three good ones," the old man said. "An awful play followed by a great play. And those great plays, they've got to give you hope."

That word again.

Charlie said, "Do you and Matt really think he's going to play better the rest of the way?"

"I do!" Joe Warren said. "I think his preseason is officially over. I think his legs are all the way underneath him now. I think he's figuring out middle linebacker a little more every week. And I think he's going to help lead us into the playoffs for the first time."

"I want you to be right about that, Mr. Warren. You have no idea how much."

"Tell you what," he said. "These doctors of mine are always telling me that having a good attitude is half the battle. I think it's actually way more than half. And if I can have a good attitude about things, so can you."

Then he told Charlie to put his arm out one more time, help him up, he wanted to go have a look at that Cold Stone his grand-daughter was always telling him about.

"Trust me on this, Charlie," the old man said. "Things are going to get better."

Thirty-Two

THE LAST THING JOE WARREN said to Charlie, after ice cream at Cold Stone and right before Charlie got out of the car in front of his house:

"I need you to at least try to make up with my hardheaded granddaughter." Grinning as he added, "Just because it will make my life a lot easier."

"Been trying, Mr. Warren."

"Try harder," he said. "Just to bring a little extra peace to an old man's life."

"She thinks I was big-timing her with Jack Sutton," Charlie said. "She said my ego got in the way."

"You think maybe it did, at least a little bit?"

"*You* think I suggested Jack to you because I wanted to get more attention than I was already getting?" Charlie said. "Because that *is* what Anna thinks."

"No, I think you did it because you thought it was the right thing for our team," Mr. Warren said. "But if you weren't a little cocky about this stuff, you wouldn't have brought him to me in the first place."

"Is cocky a good thing or bad?"

The old man grinned again and said, "Generally it's a little bit of both."

Charlie took his hand off the door. "Can I ask you something?"

"You can ask me anything," Mr. Warren said, "except where I left my slippers when I can't find them."

"Do you think I've changed?" Charlie said. "I mean, since we became friends?"

"You mean since we became boys?"

Charlie smiled. "Yes, sir. Since then."

"The answer, Charlie boy, is that you *have* changed. But not in the way my Anna—*our* Anna—seems to think. And maybe not even the way you think, if you're asking the question. But, yes, I think you have not only changed, but for the better."

"How?"

"You're more confident," Mr. Warren said. "You're more than just the boy other kids call 'Brain.'"

Charlie guessed maybe he was right. So he nodded.

Joe Warren said, "Being in the spotlight, the way you have been, that was part of it, of course. And getting knocked down a couple of pegs lately, that actually wasn't such a bad thing, either, no matter how much it hurt sometimes."

He put out his fist for the last time on this day, so Charlie could gently pound it, and said, "And maybe making yourself a new friend was part of it, too."

"The best part."

"Now go inside and call your *best* friend," the old man said. "And once you've got her on the line, do something that will never ever hurt you in your dealings with the women in your life."

"What's that?" Charlie said.

"Tell her she was right."

When he did call Anna she was on her way to a sleepover at her friend Caroline's, in the car with Caroline and her mom, saying she couldn't really talk right now.

But said, "What's up?"

"Nothing."

"You called about nothing?"

"Like I haven't done that before?"

"Good point."

"I can call you tomorrow, if you want."

Anna said, "Listen, maybe I'll call you later."

"Try not to sound so excited about it," he joked.

He had been trying to be nice, as hard as he could. There hadn't been any blowups since the big one about Jack Sutton and ego and her being a know-it-all. They'd managed to get through another *Charlie Show*. And they were having lunches together.

But things still weren't great, weren't the way they were supposed to be between them. And Charlie wanted them to be the way they used to be. Badly.

"I'll keep that advice in mind."

"I'll be up watching college football if you want to call," he said.

"I know."

"Your gramps came to my game today."

"Know that, too."

"Call me later."

"Maybe."

But sounding like for the first time in a while, she wanted things to be un-different between them herself.

His mom was at the grocery store when he walked in the house, having left a note on the counter. When she got home he told her about Mr. Warren and cancer, first thing, and they were still talking about it at dinner.

His mom telling him that one of her bosses at Sony, old but not as old as Mr. Warren, had been living with non-Hodgkin's for a long time and showed every sign of going right on living with it.

"Sometimes," she said, "diseases that sound like the worst thing in the world, because they involve cancer, move more slowly inside old people than the old people themselves move."

"For real?"

"For real. I wouldn't lie to you any more than he would."

"I still can't believe he came to the game."

"Maybe," his mom said, "Joe Warren needs somebody like you in his life as much as you need somebody like him."

Then he told her something he never had, about that day in Mr. Warren's garden when he'd told the old man about his dad and how he'd left and was never coming back; how good Mr. Warren had it with Matt even when things weren't so great.

"You said that?"

"I did," Charlie said, and told her that was the day Mr. Warren had said that he was more than just a football friend.

"Sounds like he was right."

He went into the den to watch the Alabama-Arkansas game, switching back and forth between that and Ohio State-Wisconsin. It wasn't the pros, but it was football, and it was on. There was a quarterback from Wisconsin, a junior, flying under the radar so far this season, whom Charlie thought might be able to help the Bulldogs in a couple of years.

If Mr. Warren was still listening to him about football players in a couple of years.

If Mr. Warren was still around.

Charlie thinking about that now that he was alone watching football, even if Mr. Warren acted like his illness was no biggie, making his form of cancer sound like the flu. Maybe that's what he'd really been getting at today, talking about enjoying things the way they were, enjoying what you had and not worrying about what you didn't.

One time today, when they were walking around the field, Joe Warren had said, "If the football season you were watching is the only one you were ever going to have, how much would each of the games be worth?"

If you looked at things that way, maybe the season the Bulldogs were having wasn't so terrible after all.

Anna called at halftime of the Alabama-Arkansas game. She probably knew it was halftime, being Anna, and had found a way to watch football even at Caroline's house with a bunch of other girls.

"Hey," she said.

"Hey," he said. "Where's the rest of the sleepover squad?"

"Attempting to make brownies. I am staying out of it."

Charlie heard her take the phone away and say, "Talking to Charlie, be there in a minute." Then: "Shut *up!*"

"What's happening?"

"Lots of Instagramming and Facebooking with the girls. *Lot* of video chatting."

"Maybe I should call you tomorrow."

"Why were you calling me before?"

"To tell you that you were right," he said. "And that I'm sorry."

"You'll have to be more specific. If you called me every time I was right about something, you'd need more minutes on your phone plan."

"You were right that I'd started getting too full of myself," Charlie said.

"That's not why I was mad and you know it," she said. "I was mad because you didn't tell me about Jack Sutton *before* Gramps told you not to tell me."

"I was wrong about that, too."

"Did Gramps tell you to call me?"

"He did," Charlie said. "But I was going to anyway."

"So this is all it's supposed to take, one phone call, after all the mean stuff you said to me?"

"I was a jerk that day," he said. "Hundred percent."

"You don't have to tell me, I was there, remember?"

"I did say I was sorry."

She paused and said, "My dad likes to say that sorry doesn't fix the lamp."

There was another pause and then she said, "Listen, I gotta go eat the stupid brownies now, call me tomorrow."

"Maybe we can hang around or something?"

"I'll check my schedule."

He was starting to think of a clever comeback to that when he realized that she'd already ended the call. But then Charlie knew the deal by now.

She even had to win phone calls.

Thirty-Three

THE NEXT SUNDAY THE BULLDOGS played the Rams in St. Louis. They played as if the past few weeks hadn't happened, stopping their losing streak, played as if the whole stretch of bad football had been some kind of bad dream.

Tom threw for one touchdown, ran for another, shocking everybody in the dome in St. Louis with the run, a perfect ball fake on third-and-goal from the five-yard line, fooling even his own teammates with a naked bootleg. He practically walked into the end zone for the score that made it 21–17 at the time for the Bulldogs, in a game they'd eventually win 31–20.

Big division win, as big as the loss to the Rams had been when Jack got flagged for fifteen yards at the end. But what made the win huge for Charlie was the way the team had earned it, the way the defense had gotten stops when it had to and the way the offense mixed passing and running on the last drive.

It was the kind of win that inspired hope. The kind of hope Mr. Warren was always talking about, as if hope were really the best medicine in the world for him.

Anna had agreed to come over to Charlie's house and watch the game, still not officially accepting his apology, just saying she was willing to watch the game with him and for him not to read too much into it. Once she was there, she got lost in the action the way she always did. And when the Bulldogs' last field goal put them up by eleven, she landed with such a crash jumping off his bed, Charlie's mom yelled up and asked which lamp they'd broken.

"All good, Mom," Charlie called back.

"I know the drill," she said. "Bulldogs score again."

Jack Sutton played most of the second half, was involved in a bunch of tackles, knocked down a pass on a blitz, and even got his first sack since his season debut against the Bengals. It came on third down, during the Rams' last drive of the game when they still had a shot at scoring a touchdown and tying the game at twenty-eight with a two-point conversion.

But it was more than his play. Charlie could see him, when the camera was on him, talking it up in the defensive huddle, talking it up with the defensive linemen when they were sitting on the bench. Trying to be a leader. Maybe trying to get their trust back for the big games to come.

"Forgot what it felt like for us to win a game," Charlie said when Tom Pinkett took a knee and ran out the last of the clock.

Before Anna could answer, her phone buzzed. She looked to see who it was, showed Charlie that her phone said "Gramps."

"Did I *watch*?" she said into her phone. "No, Gramps, I decided to go back and watch the whole season of *The Voice* so far. Of *course* I watched!"

She made a face and said, "Yes, I watched with Charlie." Looked at Charlie as she said, "Decided to throw him a bone."

Then she was handing Charlie the phone and he heard Joe Warren saying, "What did I tell you, Charlie boy? New season, starting right now. Brand-new season."

Charlie could hear a lot of excited chatter in the background.

"Who was it," Charlie said, "that told me all it takes is one game to change everything?"

"Some old fart," Joe Warren said. Then, "See you at practice this week?"

"Yes, sir."

"Give Anna a hug for me?"

"No, sir."

"She forgive you yet?"

"Very nice to talk to you, too, sir," Charlie said. They both laughed, and then Joe Warren told him to tell Anna he'd call her tomorrow; he was on his way down to the locker room.

The next week the Bulldogs played the Steelers at Bulldogs Stadium. The Bulldogs with a chance to get to 5–6 with five games to play, putting them a couple games out of first in a weak NFC West, trailing the 49ers and Seahawks, both tied for first place.

Charlie was back in Joe Warren's suite for that one, sitting next to the old man with the score tied at twenty, four minutes left, Bulldogs' ball.

Jack Sutton had intercepted a ball in the flat early in the game, stepping in front of the Steelers' tight end and tipping the ball to himself, grabbing it out of the air, running thirty yards to the end zone.

Like he was back running down Alvarado Street.

But he wasn't the story of this game over the last four minutes, this was just the most balanced offense the Bulldogs had shown in a while, Tom mixing short passes with runs, the Bulldogs actually running the ball more than they had in weeks, Silas Burrell doing the heavy lifting, on his way to only his second hundred-yard rushing game of the season. He ended up scoring the winning touchdown, carrying three Steelers' tacklers into the end zone.

After the touchdown, Charlie walked outside and looked around at Bulldogs Stadium going crazy, actually feeling the place shake, wondering if the players on the field could feel the *ground* shaking.

He had never seen the place so happy, never felt so connected to the rest of the fans, knowing that this was the way sports was supposed to make you feel. All in a place that had sometimes seemed not just empty of fans at this point in other seasons, but empty of life and fun.

Charlie looked at it all and heard it all and thought:

This is why Mr. Warren wanted to bring football back to his hometown.

Thirty-Four

AS NOVEMBER TURNED INTO DECEMBER, all of a sudden things had gotten a lot better in Charlie's world.

The Bulldogs were winning some games and Charlie's other team, the Culver City Cardinals, wouldn't stop winning, still solidly in first place, on their way to the league's championship game—and a rematch with Palos Verdes—if both teams held their places at number one and number two.

And things were mostly back to being the way they used to be with Anna.

The Cardinals' season would end first, one more regular season game against Pacific Palisades, and then the championship game the week after that.

At dinner one night Charlie's mom said, "It really is amazing that the Bulldogs might not have had anything close to the season they're having if it hadn't been for you."

"It's more complicated than that, Mom. Things are never that simple in sports."

"As far as I can tell, Tom Pinkett and Jack Sutton didn't bring themselves to Los Angeles."

"You know who really deserves a ton of credit?" Charlie said.

"Who?"

"Anna."

"Interesting theory. Not that I'm sure I understand it."

"Think about it, because Anna made me think about it when we were fighting," Charlie said. "She's the one who basically put me next to Mr. Warren. And if I'm not next to Mr. Warren, it doesn't matter whether I think Tom Pinkett can still play or not. She's the one who gave me the chance. She's the one who convinced me to do the podcast and to believe in myself. You've got to give her props for Tom and Jack Sutton, too."

His mom got out of her chair then, came around the table, hugged him from behind, gave him a quick kiss on top of his head, went and sat back down.

"What was that for?"

"*That*," she said, "was for being you."

The Saturday after the Bulldogs won 28–17 in Arizona with three more touchdown passes for Tom Pinkett, his total for the season putting him fourth in the league now, the Culver City Cardinals played for the championship of their league.

Rematch with Palos Verdes. Memorial Field. One vs. two. All that.

Let's go.

Anna was there with Charlie's mom, Joe Warren telling Charlie the night before that he was coming, too, wouldn't miss it, might be a little late because he had a couple of stops he had to make first, but to look for him on the Cardinals' side of the field.

"I want to hang with the winners," Joe Warren said on the phone. "Look at us, Charlie boy, both coming up winners right now, like nothing can stop either one of us."

About five minutes before the kickoff, Steve Fallon came over to Charlie and shook his hand.

"You were right about Jack Sutton," Kevin's dad, the big radio host, said. "I was wrong."

Charlie grinned and shook his head. "What do you expect from the media?"

"You know," Steve Fallon said, "I've been thinking, maybe we could do something else with you on my show besides just having you make fantasy picks."

"You'll have to talk to my agent." Charlie pointed to the bleachers.

"Your mom?" Steve Fallon said.

"Anna."

Coach Dayley came over then and said to Charlie, "You ready?"

"To play or coach?"

"How about both? How about we get one of those moments today where you know what they're going to call and then know exactly what to do about it?"

"Anything else?" Charlie said.

"No," Coach said, "that ought to do it."

Both teams lined up for the kickoff now, the Cardinals getting the ball, Charlie on the sideline. He turned and looked into the stands again, saw where his mom and Anna were sitting. Still no sign of Joe Warren. Maybe he'd gotten tied up at one of the stops he said he had to make.

And in that moment, Charlie Gaines knew something, not just in his football brain but in his heart:

He was even more excited to be here than he'd been in Bulldogs Stadium, to know he was going to be something more than a spectator. To be a part of this team, part of the day, playing in a Big Game like this.

He had come into the season without any expectations for himself, thinking of himself as a total scrub, maybe thinking of himself that way so he wouldn't be disappointed when he didn't really contribute the way his teammates did.

But things were different now, Charlie actually surprised at how fired up he was, how anxious he was to get out there, how the stakes hadn't just been raised for the Culver City Cardinals because of the way they'd played all season, but had been raised for Charlie himself.

Charlie the football player.

The second game between the two teams turned out to be even better than the first, both Jarrod and Palos Verdes' Graham Yost throwing touchdown passes in the first half, Kevin returning a punt for a touchdown, the game tied at the half, the Cardinals eventually taking a 20–19 lead into the fourth quarter.

Charlie had played the entire second quarter, just because he was doing a good job of bringing it on this day. On the Vikings' last series of the half, he'd noticed as Graham moved his fullback a little to the right of his normal setup spot, remembering they'd run the screen when Graham had moved the kid earlier. Charlie nearly got to Graham right before he released the ball, batting down the pass, just missing a sack.

But as well as he'd played, he was back next to Coach for most of the third quarter, even as Coach told him when the teams were switching sides at the end of the quarter that he was going to get him back out there.

"Cool," Charlie said, wanting to get back out there, wanting to be a player today and not just an assistant coach.

"But for now," Coach Dayley said, "keep those eyes of yours open for me."

"Always."

Every chance he got, though, he swiveled his head around and put those eyes on the bleachers, looking for Joe Warren.

Still not there.

Charlie wanting him to be here, more than he ever thought he would. Wishing that the old man had seen him knock down that pass and nearly get that sack. Wanting Mr. Warren to see something more than Charlie's football brain on display today.

Wanting him to cheer for the guy he called Charlie boy the way the dads in the stands cheered for their own boys.

With eight minutes to go in the game, Graham Yost eluded a big rush and threw a touchdown pass to his tight end. The Vikings missed on the conversion, but they now led 25–20.

Charlie watching it happen, standing next to his coach.

Coach Dayley, talking to himself more than Charlie, said, "If we really are the best team in the league, we'll be that team now."

The Cardinals didn't panic on offense, didn't try to come back all at once with long passes, played as if they had plenty of time— which they did.

Jarrod threw short passes when he wasn't handing the ball off to Kevin Fallon, Charlie sure Kevin was over a hundred rushing yards for the day now. With four minutes and forty seconds left, the Cardinals faced a third-and-four at the Vikings' seventeen-yard line. Jarrod ran an option with Kevin that had been working for them since the Cardinals' first series of the game, decided to keep the ball this time, was just about to turn the corner, plenty of open space in front of him, when the Palos Verdes safety came flying in from the side, launched himself at Jarrod, put his helmet on the ball and knocked it loose.

Fumble, scramble, big pileup.

When the refs sorted it all out, it was the Vikings' ball with time running out. A turnover might seal the win.

Coach Dayley and Coach Fallon quickly gathered the defense around them.

"We need a stop, boys," he said. "Or we need the ball. Somebody make a play for us."

The Vikings ran the ball twice for only three yards, but then Graham scrambled for nine yards and a first down.

Three minutes left.

Charlie wondering when Coach was going to call one of the

two time-outs he had left, watching the clock run, maybe running out on their season.

Graham kept it on first down, an option play, Shota Matsumoto coming up and making the play on him, a big hit that knocked Graham's right shoulder pad out of his jersey. But when everybody got up after the play, Shota stayed down, holding his shoulder. He didn't get to his feet until Coach Dayley and Coach Fallon pulled him up and started to walk him off the field.

When they all got to the sideline Coach said, "Get in there for Shota, Charlie. Don't need just your eyes now. Make a play."

The Vikings ran the ball again on second down, and Coach used his first time-out, right before the two-minute warning stopped the clock.

Third-and-long for the Vikings.

If they got another first down, the game would be over, unless the Vikings somehow turned the ball over. Game over. Season over. The Vikings—champs.

The offense broke the huddle.

As they did, the fullback started to take his normal position.

Then Graham Yost moved him to his right.

Charlie's eyes on him as he did.

Moved him the way he had in the second quarter on the screen pass Charlie had batted down.

Charlie also saw that the other running back had moved into the slot to help spread out the defense, no weak-side blocking to Graham's left if Charlie came with a blitz.

A blitz he was calling for himself now. A backup linebacker

who'd spent most of the year thinking that was his position. Backup, not linebacker.

Make a play, Coach had said.

Too late to tell anybody else—he didn't want to tip off Graham. But Charlie was sure he was going to try to throw the screen, get the first down, and close out the Cardinals right here and now.

Graham took the snap from center, Charlie so anxious he nearly jumped the count. But he was coming hard from Graham's left, nobody paying any attention to him. It was why there was suddenly all this green between Charlie and the Palos Verdes quarterback.

Jack Sutton had once said all quarterbacks, no matter how good they were, had the same chance when they didn't know you were coming.

No chance.

Charlie saw Graham Yost's arm coming up now. But he never got it moving forward.

Charlie was on him.

Making sure not to come in too high or lead with his helmet, he knew the rules about that, knew them the way his coaches did.

He kept his helmet down and lowered his shoulder and drove it into Graham's side, feeling the air come out of Graham.

The ball came loose.

Both Charlie and Graham Yost were facing the same way on the ground, right next to each other, facing the Palos Verdes end zone.

The ball was right there in front of them, maybe a yard out of their reach.

But Charlie had spotted it before Graham did and started scrambling after it like a sand crab on the beach, not wanting to waste time even trying to get to his knees.

Coach Dayley always talked about how you had to want it more than the other guy in football. Charlie wanted the football now, more than he ever wanted anything in a game he was playing and not watching.

He could see Graham out of the corner of his eye trying to get up and get to the ball, as if he had time to do both and still beat Charlie to it. Only he didn't.

Somehow in the same motion, Charlie managed to push himself up as he put his hands on the football.

He felt Graham reaching for his legs. Too late. Charlie was upright now, ball in his hands, moving, starting to run.

Running with the ball for the first time as a Culver City Cardinal.

He never even peered over his shoulder, his eyes focused only on the end zone in front of him. Never even saw all the Viking jerseys chasing him.

Not sure where he was on the field exactly, not sure if it was the twenty-yard line or the fifteen. Just seeing the end zone in front of him. Telling himself that if he was ever going to be fast, now would be as good a time as any.

He tucked the ball firmly between his elbow and shoulder, pressing it to him as hard as he could. Charlie had watched enough football in his life to have seen enough balls get knocked loose by a defender coming up from behind, the guy with the ball not expecting the hit.

The hit came when he got to the five, Charlie hearing the Palos Verdes guy yell with the effort it must have taken to catch up with him and jump on his back before it was too late.

Charlie felt the guy on him reaching for the ball. Charlie started to lose his balance and go down, knowing that even if he didn't score, he could at least put the Cardinals at the one or two, just as long as he didn't fumble and ruin the greatest play he was probably ever going to make in his life.

With one final effort, Charlie gripped the ball tight and launched himself, just trying to fall forward. He did, falling just far enough to reach the white line of the end zone.

Touchdown.

26–25 Cardinals.

The rest of the guys on defense mobbed him in the end zone.

Before they got back to the sideline Sean Barkley banged helmets with Charlie and yelled, "Brain, using his!"

The Cardinals missed the conversion. On the kickoff, the Vikings' returner took the kick back to the forty and nearly broke it for more than that, scaring Charlie and his teammates half to death.

But the Cardinals' defense held up as Graham Yost threw four straight incompletions. The Cardinals took over on downs and Jarrod knelt to run out the clock.

Game over. Cardinals the champs, by a point.

Charlie stayed on the field with his teammates, all of them waiting for the trophy presentation. Before it started, Charlie jogged over to where his mom and Anna were standing behind the Cardinals' bench.

His mom hugged him, pulled back and said, "I grew up around here. And when I was a little girl, Kirk Gibson hit this home run to win a World Series game when he was so hurt he could barely walk, and when he did the announcer said, 'I don't believe what I just saw.' Well, I'm not sure I believe what *I* just saw."

"Same," Charlie said.

Anna hit him with a high five that was so hard Charlie thought his right hand might have gone numb on him.

"I'm never calling you Brain again," she said.

"Finally."

"Only because your new nickname is Sack."

"I'll take it," he said. Then jerked his head at the bleachers and said, "Your gramps didn't make it?"

Anna smiled. "No, he made it, all right. About one minute before Sack Gaines did all kinds of bad things to the other team's quarterback."

Then she pointed toward a clump of trees beyond the bleachers, right before you got to the parking lot. Joe Warren was sitting in what looked to be some kind of fancy lawn chair, Carlos standing next to him, across from the end zone where Charlie had scored his touchdown.

Charlie ran over to Coach, asked him how long before the

trophy presentation. Coach told him he still had about five minutes, they were waiting for the photographer to get here.

"Go say hi to the owner," Coach said.

"You know he's here?"

"We always know when he's here, Charlie."

Mr. Warren made no move to get out of the chair when Charlie got to him. Charlie could see why; the old man looked as tired as he had ever seen him.

But still smiling through it.

"You saw?" Charlie said. "Anna said you got here in time to see."

"I saw, Charlie boy," the old man said. "Saw as good a defensive play as I've seen all season, is what I saw. Even better than the one our friend Sack Sutton made the other game."

"We both saw," Carlos said.

"Well," the owner of the L.A. Bulldogs said, "now you've got one more football title than I do."

"For now," Charlie said. "Who's the one always telling me how much football there is left to be played? Help me out here."

"Some old fart," the old man said. "A real tired one."

Even his voice sounding weak today.

Joe Warren put his arm out now, pointing out at the field, the league championship trophy on a table at midfield, Coach Dayley and Coach Fallon already out there, along with most of the players, Charlie knowing he had to get out there himself.

"I'm also the one always telling you to enjoy all our Sundays, Charlie," Mr. Warren said. "But I forget to tell you the same goes for these Saturdays of yours, too. Because someday you're going to look back on them and think you'd give everything you own to just get one of them back." He took a deep breath, as if he were the one who'd just run for the winning score. "Now go get your trophy."

Charlie leaned down next to him and said, "Today wouldn't have been nearly as great if you hadn't seen that play."

"Great for both of us," Mr. Warren said. Then gave him a little shove and said, "Now *git*."

Carlos helped him out of his chair. When he was standing he said to Carlos, "I believe I can take it from here."

Carlos smiled at Charlie. "*Yes*, sir," he said.

Carlos walked a few yards toward the field with Charlie, saying, "We were late because we had to stop at the hospital."

Charlie looked up at him. "Is he okay?"

"Now he is," Carlos said.

Charlie ran the rest of the way toward the field. Before he got to where his teammates were standing, he took one last look over his shoulder, saw Joe Warren smiling at him, waving.

And for that one moment he didn't look old or sick or tired, just as happy as Charlie felt.

Maybe that wasn't better than a championship, or a championship trophy, or even being called Sack Gaines on this day.

But it was close enough.

Thirty-Five

CHARLIE WASN'T EVEN SURE IF he understood it—he just assumed there were things you never understood about yourself, no matter how old you were—but he felt less alone now, even when he was by himself. More a part of something than he'd ever been before.

Like a large family.

It was like football had taken him in as much as Mr. Warren and his team had.

Charlie Gaines had never thought of himself as some sad, lonely kid because he didn't have a dad in his life, even if he'd always been a little jealous of kids who did have dads. And he'd always known how lucky he was to have a mom like his, one who didn't try too hard to be both mom *and* dad, just wanted to be the best mom she could be for Charlie: cool and smart and loving and somehow always there for him when he needed her, even though she had a full-time job.

She didn't try to bluff her way through on sports stuff she didn't know. She was just herself. Maybe that was the coolest thing about her. She was totally comfortable being herself.

Then Mr. Warren came along.

Somehow Joe Warren, without acting as if he wanted to be Charlie's dad or even his granddad, had done about as much as anybody could have done to fill up that hole in his life. What he had always thought of as an empty room. The old man was there for Charlie because he *wanted* to be there. When Anna had asked Charlie that time how he liked being a member of the Warren family, she had just been trying to be funny, or snarky, or both.

But Charlie knew the answer now, knew that he liked it just fine. He liked being an honorary Warren, knowing that if he wasn't related to Joe Warren he was connected to him in a way he'd never been connected to a grown-up man in his life.

Honorary Warren, honorary Bulldog. All one family now inside Charlie's head. His team really becoming *his* in a way he never thought possible.

It was the Wednesday after Christmas. Bulldogs' practice before the second-to-last game of the regular season. Both of their final games were at home, first against the Cowboys, and then against the Seahawks.

Fresh off of five straight victories, the Bulldogs were now 8-6, tied for first in the NFC West with the Seahawks.

If the Seahawks beat the Eagles on Saturday night and the Bulldogs beat the Cowboys on Sunday, the Bulldogs would be playing for their first division title, at home, eleven days from now.

The way the rest of the conference looked, neither the Bulldogs nor the Seahawks would get a wildcard at 9–7, so the winner of the game, if this weekend's games played out right, would go to the playoffs and the loser would go home. If Seattle won on Saturday night, the Bulldogs would be playing knockout-tournament-like ball for two straight Sundays, like the playoffs were starting for them right then.

Considering where the team was when it was losing four in a row, when it looked to be going nowhere, a chance like this was the real dream.

He and Mr. Warren had watched practice from the field today, Jack Sutton coming over at one point and saying, "Hey, I heard somewhere that now you've turned into a bit of a sack artist yourself."

Charlie looked at Mr. Warren, who said, "I can't imagine where he would have heard something like that."

"I don't think one career sack makes you a sack *artist* exactly," Charlie said.

"Whatever," Jack said. "I just wanted to come over and say I owed you one. A big one."

"Get me two more wins and we'll call it even."

When practice was over Mr. Warren said he wanted to talk to

Coach Fiore in his office for a few minutes, but if Charlie was ready to go, he could have somebody find Carlos. Charlie said no, he was good, he'd just hang around until Mr. Warren finished his meeting.

"I like it down here," Charlie said.

"I picked up on that," the old man said, and then began his slow walk toward the tunnel.

Charlie went and sat on the bench. After all this time, he still couldn't believe he *was* here, even with all the players and coaches now in the locker room . Like Charlie had the place to himself.

He was still on the bench when he heard a voice behind him say, "About time we had a talk."

Turned around and saw that it was Matt Warren.

Even this far into the season, after everything that had happened—and as much as Charlie was around Bulldogs Stadium—he hardly had any kind of relationship with Matt Warren.

Oh, Matt would say hello and ask how he was doing when Charlie was on the field, or in his dad's office, or when Matt would stop by his dad's suite during a home game, even though the Bulldogs had mostly been on the road lately. He would also be polite and try to act friendly. And, as Charlie would tell himself, there was absolutely no reason for him to do anything more than that, whether Charlie had gotten as close as he had to Joe Warren or not.

And maybe there would always be some weirdness between them, Matt being the general manager and the owner's son and the future big boss of everything, and Charlie being this kid who'd stolen the headlines when he'd found the team a quarterback and a middle linebacker they so desperately needed.

Matt and Charlie both knowing, without ever having had a conversation about it, that the Bulldogs would probably have had no shot at making the playoffs without those guys.

Charlie hoping that Matt didn't want to have that conversation now, the one he'd had plenty of times with Anna about her uncle.

Anna saying one time, "You know how when people avoid a subject and say there's an elephant in the room? You and my uncle have, like, a whole *circus*."

Now here they both were, just the two of them.

"Mind if I pull up a seat?" Matt Warren said, sitting down next to Charlie on the bench.

Dressed the way he was usually dressed—khakis and a button down shirt and Nike sneakers in Bulldog blue—when he was on the field for practice, walking around, all business, going from coach to coach, sometimes talking to players, like this was his real office, not the one upstairs.

"Kind of neat when the place is empty like this," Matt said, "isn't it?"

"Totally."

They both sat staring straight ahead, Charlie feeling suddenly quite small.

"Can I tell you something, Charlie?"

"Sure, Mr. Warren."

"Please . . . We went over this before. My dad is Mr. Warren. Call me Matt."

"Sure . . . Matt."

"At first," Matt said, "I didn't want you around."

Here we go, Charlie thought.

"You don't seem surprised."

"Not really."

"But now I'm glad you're around, and not just because you made a couple of calls that even the smartest personnel guys in the league might not have made. Including our own."

"Probably because it's not my job," Charlie said. "You guys are the ones under all the pressure, every single week. Since I've been around the team like this, I went back and looked at all the draft choices you've made, especially the lower ones." Charlie paused and said, "You've done way better than people think."

Matt grinned. "People like my niece, you mean?"

"Seriously," Charlie said. "I like to think I follow things *really* closely with the Bulldogs. But when I started going over the decisions you've made, year by year, I can see how people have focused on the stuff that didn't work out more than the things that did."

"That's the job, Charlie, at least until you win," Matt said. "And then sometimes even *after* you've won. *I* know what I can do. *I* know I'm a better general manager than all those people you're talking about think. But my job isn't to turn *them* around, it's to get this team turned around. Which I think we've finally done."

"People who only focus on Tom coming here this season aren't seeing the whole picture, are they?"

Matt grinned and shook his head. "Nope. But it's like my dad told me one time: Sports fans just see the hole in the donut. Not the whole donut."

"Can I ask you something?" Charlie said.

"Ask me anything."

"How come you don't defend yourself more? Your record, I mean."

"Because I'm a Bill Parcells guy all the way. His most famous line was the one about how you are what your record says you are. And everybody can see what our record has been since we were an expansion team."

"I got criticized over Jack Sutton and I didn't want to come out of my room," Charlie said. "I read the papers and listen to the radio and go on the Internet and it's like, wow, you have to take it all the time."

"But if you get fixed on it, then you're taking time away from doing your job," Matt said. "And my job, more than anything else, is to build a winner, for our fans. Mostly for my dad."

Charlie looking at Matt now like he was seeing him for the first time.

"I really didn't think you liked me very much," Charlie said. "Especially when Jack was messing up big time."

"Like I said, there were times . . . But guess what? That was so dumb it made me not like *me*."

Then: "Take a walk with me, Charlie."

And so now Charlie began a walk around another football field, this time with Joe Warren's son at Bulldogs Stadium.

"I'm just glad those guys worked out for us," Charlie said.

"Not as glad as I am," Matt said. "All I've ever wanted to do was put together a team like this. Not just a quarterback who can get it done, or a linebacker who's found a second chance. But all over the field, up and down the depth chart. But those two players, they really fit like missing pieces to a puzzle. I guess what I'm trying to say is that I never officially thanked you for what you did to help the team. I am thanking you now."

"I was never looking for a thank-you. I used to just want the Bulldogs to win for me, because it would make me happy. But now I want it even more for your dad."

"That makes us more alike than either one of us would have ever thought, huh?"

They had gone up the Bulldogs' side of the field, crossed the end zone, were heading down the visitors' side now.

"You know what that means?" Matt said. "You and I—we were always on the same team."

Then he paused and said, "He told me he told you about being sick."

"Yeah."

"So now he's a happy guy who happens to be sick," Matt said. "Which is why it's a good thing that you help make him even happier. I watch the two of you and you both make being around each other look so . . . *easy*. Makes me wish it had always been that easy between us. My dad and me."

They kept walking, Charlie saying, "He tells me all the time how proud he is of you. How he knows how hard it is for you being the owner's son. The other day he was saying again how none of this would have been as much fun for him if the two of you weren't doing this together. Even in the bad times."

There was a stray football in the grass in front of them that the equipment guys had somehow missed. Matt picked it up and then surprised Charlie by getting off a booming punt—crushed it—that traveled fifty yards in the air at least.

"Seriously?" Charlie said.

"Once I realized in college I was never going to be good enough to make the NFL as a player, I started kicking, thinking I could punt my way there. That was long before the Bulldogs. Made it through a couple of cuts with the Cardinals before I got sent home."

They started walking again, Charlie not sure how long they'd been out there, or what time it was. Just enjoying the talk more than he'd thought he would.

"When Dad got sick," Matt Warren said, "I started to wonder if I had even less time than I thought to get this team figured out. Not so much in the draft, that's a crapshoot even for general managers a lot smarter than I am. I'm talking about some of the quick-fix trades I made." He paused and blew out some air and said, "There's this old racetrack expression: Scared money never wins. I was getting more and more scared that I was running out of time with him."

"I get jumpy just making fantasy trades!"

They were back at the Bulldogs' bench now. They both sat back down. Matt looked at his watch. "Dad should be out any second."

"Thanks for the talk," Charlie said.

"Should have had it sooner."

Then Matt said, "Here comes the big guy."

There was Joe Warren, coming out of the tunnel, walking as slowly and carefully as before, as if afraid the turf might reach up and bring him down.

Don't fall, Charlie heard him saying.

"One last thing, Charlie?" Matt said. "It turned out to be good for me that you were around, too. Because I learned something from you."

"I doubt that."

"No, I did. I figured out that one of the reasons you get on the way you do with Dad is because you don't need anything from him, the way I've always needed his approval."

Charlie was about to tell him that he was wrong, that he needed Joe Warren—needed all of this, the team and the place and all the rest of it—more than Matt could ever know.

But now Joe Warren was walking up to the bench area, saying, "Well, look at my brain trust."

"Yeah," Matt said, looking at Charlie and grinning. "Look at us. Couple of brains."

Thirty-Six

MR. WARREN'S SUITE, BULLDOGS AGAINST the Cowboys, Seattle having already won its game the night before and taking its record to 9–6, Bulldogs needing a win to match.

If the Bulldogs lost to the Cowboys they would be out of the playoffs. Even if they beat the Seahawks next week to split the season series, the Seahawks still had the tiebreaker on the Bulldogs because of a better record in their division.

It was really win or go home for the Bulldogs as far as the playoffs were concerned.

As the Bulldogs tried to get Joe Warren into the playoffs for the first time.

Charlie wanted this for himself, wanted it as much as he'd ever wanted anything in sports. This was his team, the only team he'd ever rooted for, his team now more than it had ever been. And he wanted this for Anna, too. And for Tom Pinkett, having had this kind of season when most people in football thought he wasn't going to have any season at all.

Charlie wanted it for Jack Sutton, not only having made a

comeback out of retirement, but now making a comeback from the way his first comeback had started.

But Charlie knew in his heart he wanted it for the old man most of all.

He *was* Brain when it came to football, whether he liked people calling him that or not. But not a brain about everything, certainly not about doctors or medicine or illness. He also wasn't an idiot about those things. So he knew that just because Mr. Warren said the cancer wasn't going to kill him anytime soon, that didn't mean that it wouldn't.

Less than two minutes left in the half, the Bulldogs were losing to the Dallas Cowboys, 24–7.

They weren't playing all that badly. It wasn't lousy play that had put them in this kind of hole. More like lousy luck. There had been a punt return for a touchdown. There had been what looked to be a sure interception by one of the Bulldogs' cornerbacks that ricocheted off the corner's hands directly into the hands of the Cowboys' tight end, who spun around and found himself with nothing but green field between him and the end zone thanks to one of the Bulldogs' safeties, who had slipped on the turf as he changed direction on the run.

"*This,*" Anna said, "is not the way the story is supposed to go."

Before her grandfather could say anything, she turned and pointed a finger at him and said, "And please don't tell me there's a long way to go."

Joe Warren hadn't moved much since he'd taken his usual seat between Charlie and Anna, his "lucky" seat not very lucky so far, the old man looking every bit as exhausted as he had been every time Charlie had seen him lately.

All he did now was wink at Charlie. As if that was all he had in him, other than a weak smile.

Somehow Charlie knew what he wanted him to say.

"There *is* a long way to go," he said to Anna.

"Very funny," Anna said.

But her gramps said, "You didn't say anything about Charlie saying it."

"If we can manage a touchdown here," Charlie said, "we can close out the half with some momentum. And then we'll get the ball to start the second half with a chance to get right back in the game."

"And what makes you think that's going to happen the way things have been going for us today?"

Now Charlie was the one giving Joe Warren a wink. "Trust."

That word again.

Three plays later, after an interference call against the Cowboys at their five-yard line, Tom Pinkett threw to Mo Bettencourt, the tight end who'd become his favorite receiver, and the Bulldogs were down only ten.

"Game on," Charlie said as the first half clock expired.

Then Isaac Powell nearly took the opening kick of the second half back all the way, before being knocked out of bounds on the Dallas thirty-eight by their kicker. Tom didn't waste much time from there—throwing immediately into the end zone, where

Harrison Mays outjumped what looked like the entire Dallas secondary to make it 24–21.

"Game *so* on," Charlie said as the crowd erupted. Even Anna jumped and whooped with excitement.

Charlie looked at Mr. Warren, but he was quiet. Not even a joke or a wink. Instead he just coughed into his hand, a weak-sounding noise that frightened Charlie.

When Charlie and Anna made a popcorn trip early in the third quarter he said to her, "I'm worried about your gramps."

"I know, me too. But when I asked my mom, she said it's just more about him acting his age finally than being sick. Mom calls it the same old same old, emphasis on the *old*." She smiled, but Charlie could tell it was forced.

They went back to their seats without saying another word. The Bulldogs stopped scoring now, but so did the Cowboys, the third quarter all defense. The fourth quarter began the same way, neither team able to push the ball past midfield.

Until Jake Kincaid, the Cowboys' second-year quarterback out of Baylor, made a great play getting out of what should have been a Sack Sutton sack, ran to his right, and threw one as far as he could to Zak Connolly for the touchdown that made it 31–21 Cowboys, five minutes left.

The stadium grew quiet again, as quiet as it had been at 24–7, like somebody had hit the mute button.

Except for Anna Bretton, who leaned past her grandfather and said in a loud voice to Charlie, "Two-score game. Remind me again: I was supposed to trust you about *what*, exactly?"

"We need a quick score" was all Charlie had. "Score and a stop."

They got the score, Tom Pinkett going into his two-minute offense a few minutes early working the sidelines with short passes, needing to use only one of the time-outs he had left, and finally taking the ball in himself on a sneak with two minutes and twenty seconds left to make it 31–28 Cowboys at Bulldogs Stadium.

Charlie looked over and saw Anna squeezing her grandfather's hand. It was going to be one of those wild finishes that every football fan loves, win or lose.

After the kickoff, the Cowboys ran it on first down, trying to run off some clock. Coach Fiore called the Bulldogs' final time-out, using it before the two-minute warning. The Cowboys ran it again on second down. Four more yards.

Third-and-four, clock running, no way for the Bulldogs to stop it. Just needing a stop to get the ball back. A first down would mean the game was over.

"He's gonna throw for it," Charlie said.

"Oh, great, Gramps," Anna said. "He's having another one of his visions."

"Nope," Charlie said. "Not seeing the future, just the season Tom Pinkett has had. The Cowboys have seen it, too. They know that even without time-outs, even a minute is too much time for him. They can't take the chance on another run."

"Any other brilliant observations?" Anna said.

It was then that Joe Warren spoke, in a soft voice.

"This young quarterback Jake Kincaid, who's lit up the

scoreboard for them all season, he never plays it safe, no matter what the score," the old man said. "He doesn't want to ask his defense to end the game. He wants to end it right here."

Mr. Warren and Charlie were both right.

It was a pass play.

A safe one, to Connolly, two yards past the first-down marker—a neat, simple curl.

That was the way it was drawn up, anyway, the way it was supposed to go, until Jack Sutton came flying in from Jake Kincaid's back side, got to him even though the Cowboys' fullback tried to put a good block on him.

Jack Sutton ran right through that block and hit Kincaid the way Charlie had hit Graham Yost at Memorial Field.

And knocked the ball loose just as Kincaid's arm came forward, the ball going straight up into the air before landing in the arms of Chuck Stoner, the Bulldogs' outside linebacker. Stoner made sure to wrap his arms around the ball before most of the Cowboys' offensive line fell on him.

Chuck had gotten the interception.

But Jack had made it happen.

The next thing everybody at Bulldogs Stadium saw was Jack Sutton pointing up at Joe Warren's suite, like he was pointing right at the old man.

Like that play was for him alone.

There was some drama right after that, a holding call on first down that pushed the Bulldogs back to the Cowboys' thirty-five and put them in a first-and-twenty situation. Then Tom nearly threw an interception on second down that tried to end the game and stop Charlie's heart at the same time.

But then Tom threw a couple of perfect balls to get the Bulldogs inside the Cowboys' ten-yard line with twenty seconds left, time running out. The players ran to the line of scrimmage as fast as they could. Everyone on both teams—every person watching in the stadium and on TV—knew what was coming next. Tom Pinkett had to spike the ball to stop the clock and prepare for one shot at the end zone.

Only, that's not what he did.

Instead, he faked the spike, pulling the ball back up like it was a yo-yo on a string before turning and faking a throw to Mo Bettencourt on his right, only to whip around and fire a strike to a wide-open Harrison Mays in the left corner of the end zone.

Touchdown. The defense never knew what hit them.

But the game was over. Along with the Cowboys' season.

It took a while, but Joe Warren finally got himself up and out of his chair with a little help from Charlie and Anna, hugged his granddaughter, then turned to Charlie and hugged him, too. For the first time. Pulling him in and saying, "I told you great things can still happen."

Then he said, "C'mon, you two, it's a special occasion, let's all of us go downstairs to the locker room."

Carlos was waiting for them at Joe Warren's private elevator, a security guard with him. Another security guard was waiting for them when the doors opened at the basement level of Bulldogs

Stadium. They all walked at the old man's pace down a long hall-way to the door that led to the home team's locker room.

"Be back for you in a bit," Joe Warren said as Carlos held the door open for him and he disappeared through it.

"Got a little pep in his step now," Charlie said.

"I think pep might be a bit strong," Anna said. "But I'll take it."

About ten minutes later the same door opened and Joe Warren came back through it.

He wasn't alone.

No security flanking him this time, just Tom Pinkett and Jack Sutton.

Jack with a football in his hands.

He said to Charlie, "Tom and I were talking inside after the rest of the team gave me this game ball. Mostly talking about how the two of us ended up here. And how *neither* one of us would have ended up here if it hadn't been for you."

He handed the ball to Charlie.

"I thanked you one time for believing in me," Tom Pinkett said. "Thanks for believing in both of us."

"I don't know what to say," Charlie said. In that moment, all he could muster was a simple thank-you.

"No," Jack said. "Thank *you*."

"I can really keep this?"

"You better, kid," Jack Sutton said. "Told you I owed you one.

Thirty-Seven

THREE HOURS LATER, AFTER DINNER, Charlie got out of his mom's car, and promised her he wouldn't be long. He ran up the walkway, pretending he was a star running back, rang the doorbell.

When Anna Bretton opened her front door, Charlie handed her the game ball.

He had rehearsed what he was going to say on the way over, knowing he better keep it short, hoping he wouldn't choke it down when he started talking.

Choke it down being one of her expressions.

"None of this would have happened without you," Charlie said. "Without you believing in me."

Anna just stared at him with big eyes. The biggest.

"The thing is," he said, "I might have been Brain to everybody else. But I knew I was always more than that to you."

Then he said, "I know sorry doesn't always fix the lamp. But I hope this ball does."

"Now," Anna said, "I'm the one who doesn't know what to say."

Charlie smiled then. "Finally."

It was when he got home that she called and told him her grandfather had been rushed to the hospital.

Thirty-Eight

ANNA'S MOM SPOKE WITH CHARLIE'S mom from the hospital, explaining what had happened.

Charlie listening on the extension.

Hearing Mrs. Bretton talk about the chest pains Mr. Warren got when he came home from the game, the shortness of breath, Carlos seeing the blood he'd coughed up in the sink when he found Joe Warren on the bathroom floor and called 911.

Mrs. Bretton saying how fast the emergency people from Cedars-Sinai Medical Center had gotten to the house, as if they somehow knew how much money her father had given to the hospital in his life.

"They're doing more tests," she said, "but they're fairly certain it was a clot in his lung that caused everything. The official language is pulmonary embolism, which is fairly common in people his age with non-Hodgkin's."

Neither one of them said anything until Mrs. Bretton said in a soft voice, "It's not good."

"He's a fighter," Charlie's mom said.

"Say a prayer," Anna's mom said. "Tell Charlie to say one, too. They gave him a shot of heavy-hitter blood thinners, which act as clot busters. Getting him to the hospital as fast as they did helped a lot. Carlos was right there with him the whole way."

Finally: "I'll be here through the night, if anything changes is it all right to call?"

"Of course."

"The next few hours . . ." Mrs. Bretton said, and that's as far as she got before she ended the call.

Charlie came into the kitchen.

"He can't die, Mom," he said. "He can't."

She walked over and put her arms around him. "You heard her. They're doing everything they can."

"This was the best day he ever had in football," Charlie said. "Now it's turned into the worst."

"She said she'd call with any news."

"Bad news, you mean," Charlie said.

"We don't know that. And can't assume the worst."

"He can't die," Charlie said.

They stood there, neither one of them moving, until she said, "I know nothing can take your mind off this. But isn't there a game on you were going to watch, so you don't sit here the rest of the night waiting for the phone to ring?"

"I don't care about football tonight," he said.

"Didn't say you had to care, honey. Just use it for company." She kissed the top of his head.

He went into the den and tried to watch the rest of the Ravens-Colts game, trying to get involved. Another one of Anna's favorite expressions. *Get involved, Gaines,* she'd say when she was excited about something and wanted him to be excited, about a TV show or movie or song or even a new flavor at Cold Stone.

All these images from the game on TV and the only image he had was Mr. Warren in some hospital bed, a bunch of tubes attached to him. Waiting for a call from Anna. A text. Something.

Then thinking that maybe he didn't want any of those things, because the next news would be bad.

Or even the worst.

Sitting there with this game on in front of him and thinking of the game at Bulldogs Stadium this afternoon, Mr. Warren hugging him and telling him, one more time, that great things could still happen.

Now all Charlie wanted to happen was for his friend to make it through the night.

He wasn't sure if he'd fallen asleep or was about to fall asleep, as if everything that had happened today and tonight had finally caught up with him, when he felt his phone buzzing next to his pillow.

Anna.

He's doing a little better.

Charlie texted her right back.

For real?

Anna, right back at him.

For real. Woke up. Talking.

Charlie again.

Awesome!

Anna, one last time.

Said for me to give you a message:

Said for you to trust him this time.

Thirty-Nine

CHARLIE WASN'T ALLOWED TO SEE him until Thursday afternoon.

Joe Warren had done well the first two days in the hospital but then there had been more clotting on Tuesday night and into Wednesday morning, Charlie not finding out until Anna called him before school.

So he had spent another day and night in the intensive care unit before they moved him into a private room on Thursday morning, telling him he would be staying in the hospital at least through the weekend, which meant through the Seattle game on Sunday.

Anna and Charlie waited outside school for Carlos to pick them up and take them to Cedars-Sinai, Carlos a little late because he'd caught some traffic.

"Any other week I wouldn't be thinking about anything *but* the big game on Sunday," Anna said. "Now Gramps isn't just the big game, he's the only game."

"He's become what he always says the Bulldogs are in L.A.," Charlie said. "Only game in town. Just not the way he ever wanted to be."

When they got to Cedars-Sinai they signed in at the front desk along with Carlos and then checked in at the nurses' station when they got up to Joe Warren's floor.

For what felt like the twentieth time since they'd left school Anna told Charlie to be prepared, he didn't just look weak, it was like his skin had turned this weird shade of gray.

"I got this," Charlie said.

He didn't. Joe Warren looked even weaker than Anna said he did. Smaller somehow. But Charlie bluffed his way through, smiled at the old man, who smiled back. "Hey there, Charlie boy," he said, nodding at Anna. "Who's your friend?"

"You must be feeling better," Anna said, "now it's only your sense of humor that is weak."

She did most of the talking, something Charlie knew she always did when she was nervous. Or scared. Going on and on about the Seattle game, how she and Charlie were going to bring it home, how she knew her old gramps was going to be out of here and back in his lucky chair when the Bulldogs played in their very first playoff game.

When she finally ran down the way a windup toy does, Joe Warren managed another weak smile.

"And how did your day go, Charlie?" he said.

"Oh, I get it," Anna said. "Bust on the girl. You guys stay here and have your little fun while Carlos and I go get a snack, it's been ages since I had anything to eat."

"Probably an hour, tops," Charlie said.

At the door she turned and said, "Try not to miss me too much."

When she was gone her grandfather said, "I believe that girl could power my stadium if the lights ever went out the way they did that time at the Super Bowl."

Charlie said, "If she didn't blow all the fuses herself."

Mr. Warren patted the side of his bed and said, "Pull up a little closer so I don't feel like I'm shouting."

Even though his voice hadn't been much more than a raspy whisper.

When Charlie had his chair as close as he could get it to the bed, the old man said, "You doing okay?"

It got a laugh out of Charlie, even here, even in a hospital room. He hated hospitals, hated everything about them, starting with the smell.

"How am *I* doing?" he said.

"Minute you walked in, it was like you'd seen a ghost," the old man said. "*Me.*"

Charlie thinking there were probably ghosts who looked better than Joe Warren did right now, with all of those tubes hooked up to the monitor next to him.

"You have to get better!" Charlie said now, feeling as if he was the one shouting, the words just coming out.

"I *am* getting better," Joe Warren said, "though probably not as fast as you or I would want. Told you old people go slow."

"Don't do what you always tell me not to do and just tell me what you think I want to hear."

Joe Warren slowly raised his arm, like it had a weight attached to it, formed a fist, reached over so Charlie could bump it with his own.

"I'm not afraid to die, Charlie. I've never been afraid to die." Now he winked. "I've just informed my doctors that I'd prefer not to do it *now*."

He reached over and covered Charlie's hand with his own, the way he'd done with Anna when she was sitting next to the bed, his hand feeling as if it had been packed in ice.

"From the time I came down with this disease of mine," the old man said, "I've had to take stock of my life, Charlie. Add it up, like putting points on the board. It's what everybody does when they get as old as I am. Did I do everything I wanted, make a difference in the world, do right by my family? And no matter what regrets I came up with, the bottom line was always the same, that I'm the luckiest sonofagun I know."

"I'm the lucky one," Charlie said. "Having you as my friend."

Joe Warren had a brief coughing fit then, Charlie not liking the rough sound of it. When it ended, Mr. Warren pointed to the water glass on the table next to him. Charlie handed him the glass, and Joe Warren leaned forward and drank from it.

"What were we saying?"

"How lucky we both are."

"Oh, yes. You want to know what the worst part of the losing was, in all the other years? How bad my family felt for me. They'd feel bad for me and I'd feel even worse for them, and then I'd remind them that there are only thirty-three of these teams on the planet, and if you can't have fun owning one, even in the bad times, then maybe you just don't know how to have fun."

"Everybody was having fun until you landed here," Charlie said.

"And we're going to keep having fun," the old man said. "All of us. Starting with the two of us."

"You promise?"

"Cross my heart and hope to live as long as your friend Anna says I'm going to."

Charlie was sure Carlos and Anna were back by now, probably waiting outside. It was their way of letting him have some extra time with Joe Warren.

"You know what I'd like to do before you leave?" he said to Charlie. "I'd like to talk a little football."

And so they talked football the way they did when their friendship really began. Like they were over at Bulldogs Stadium, up in his office, looking down at practice.

When they were finally talked out, Charlie just stayed where he was next to the bed, still holding Mr. Warren's hand, the room quiet now except for the beeps of the monitor. The old man was breathing easily now, eyes closed, asleep.

Now Charlie was the one talking in a whisper. "Please don't die."

And just like that, Joe Warren opened his eyes.

"No more talk about dying," he said, giving Charlie's hand one more squeeze. "Just remember one more promise I made you about the day we make the playoffs."

"I forget," Charlie said to him.

"You still haven't seen me dance," the old man said.

Forty

MORNING OF THE BIG GAME, Charlie awake at seven o'clock, watching the pregame shows on ESPN and the NFL network, switching from channel to channel until he found somebody talking about Bulldogs vs. Seahawks, trying to learn something about the game he didn't already know himself.

At nine o'clock, the Fox pregame show came on, Terry Bradshaw doing an interview with Matt Warren, Matt telling him that he couldn't believe that after all the years when the Bulldogs were just playing out the string and already thinking about next year's draft on the last Sunday of the regular season, here they were in the big game and his dad would be watching from a hospital.

"At least we've arranged to have his lucky chair from his suite set up in his hospital room," Matt said.

Anna called when the interview was over, saying even she didn't know about the lucky chair, then saying, "I can't wait all day for this game!"

"Usually I care about all the games," Charlie said. "But today I only care about one."

"Pretend you're just following all your fantasy teams," she said. "That will keep your mind occupied."

"Yeah," Charlie said. "If I get enough catches out of Mo Bettencourt, I can even win that head-to-head league from that Dream Team guy. I've pretty much already won all the other leagues."

"Good, focus on that. I'll see you later in our lucky seats. It's going to be fun."

Charlie was in front of the big screen in his den watching the early game, Redskins-Cowboys, when his phone buzzed, a phone number Charlie didn't recognize, and then Charlie heard Joe Warren's voice saying, "Happy Sunday, Charlie boy."

"How you feeling, Mr. Warren?"

"Feeling like I should be at my own stadium watching my own team—that's how I'm feeling."

Charlie wanted to tell him that the way the week began, he was just happy the old man was watching at all, but just said, "Totally not fair."

"But that's not why I'm calling," the old man said. "I'm just calling to tell you to make sure you remember every part of this day when you get to the stadium, from the time Carlos walks you in. You got it?"

"Got it."

"You be my eyes and ears one more time, okay?"

"Okay."

"We're gonna make a memory today, Charlie," he said. "Even though you'll be there, and I'll be here, we're still a team."

"No team I'd rather be on," Charlie said, smiling as he put down the phone. Brain, feeling like one again on the last Sunday of the regular season.

Feeling brilliant all of a sudden, like he could see the whole day unfolding exactly the way it was supposed to.

Anna and her mom and her uncle Matt had to be at the stadium early to do an interview with Bob Costas about Joe Warren that was going to air at halftime.

Mr. Warren had arranged for Carlos to pick up Charlie and take him to the game at three o'clock. If the Bulldogs won and made the playoffs, Anna and her mom and Charlie would all go celebrate with Mr. Warren in the hospital.

"The after-party," Anna said to Charlie in their third or fourth phone conversation of the day.

"I'll think about after-parties after we've won the game," Charlie said.

"I can't wait to be in my seat," Anna said.

"Me neither."

Carlos was out in front of Charlie's house at five minutes to three, and as soon as Charlie had his seat belt buckled, they were talking about the game, what they thought the keys would be, like they were their own pregame show. And Carlos talked about how he had only ever dreamed about what Bulldogs Stadium would feel like and sound like for a game like this.

"Me too," Charlie said. Then he asked if they could change the subject for a minute.

Carlos smiled. "Is there anything else in the world to talk about today?"

Charlie told him.

"Really?" Carlos said.

"Really."

Fifteen minutes later Carlos dropped him off at the hospital.

"You're sure this is where you want to watch the game?" Carlos said.

"Exactly where I want to watch."

Next to Joe Warren's lucky chair, just like always.

Forty-One

"CARLOS HAD ASKED IF HE could keep me company," Joe Warren said to Charlie. "And I told him no, he should be at the stadium, where you should be, young man."

"I'd rather be with you."

"You should be at the stadium, today of all days."

"I should be with you," Charlie said. "Today of all days."

Then the old man smiled.

"And I with you, Charlie boy. And I with you." He sighed and said, "We'll deal with the fallout from my granddaughter later."

"I already texted her," Charlie said. "And you know what she said back?"

"Not a clue."

"She said I was right."

"How can we lose today," Joe Warren said, "if a miracle like that can happen?"

■ ■ ■

It was 10–10 midway through the second quarter, Tom Pinkett and Colt Marley, the Seahawks' QB, each having thrown for a touchdown pass, each having been picked off once, the game more of a defensive battle so far than anything else. Jack Sutton already had two sacks, was playing the best game he'd played so far, making things pretty miserable for Colt Marley every time he got near the Seahawks' backfield.

"You know we would've had no shot at first place without him?" Joe Warren said. "Not to inflate that ego of yours Miss Anna is always worrying about."

"You don't know that for sure, Mr. Warren. Fallacy of the predetermined outcome."

"You listen too well, Mr. Boy General Manager."

Charlie said, "Assistant boy GM."

"One thing you can see today from Sack Sutton," Joe Warren said. "He's not afraid of the occasion. You look at some of these guys, both teams, you'd have trouble pulling a needle out of their backsides with a tractor."

Just trying to picture it made Charlie laugh. When he stopped he said, "You know he's never made the playoffs, either. This might be the best chance *he's* ever going to get."

It was as though Jack Sutton could smell the playoffs and was determined to carry the whole team on his back if he had to. Which is what made what happened next so hard to watch.

Seahawks driving, third-and-eight from the Bulldogs' thirty, Colt Marley passing from the pocket for a change, or trying to, before he was flushed out by defensive pressure.

Jack Sutton was the one chasing him, running in that moment as if the season was making him younger rather than older.

Marley, running to his right, turned upfield to evade the pass rush and saw he had a chance to make a lot more than eight yards and a first down.

Marley cut back suddenly toward the middle of the field, clearly seeing he could pick up a block on Jack from his tight end.

Everything was happening at once now, the tight end crashing into Jack and taking him down just as he was reaching for Colt Marley, Ray Milner flying in from the other side like it was Marley's blind side in that moment, knocking the ball loose.

There was a big scramble for the ball, a huge pileup in the middle of Bulldogs Stadium.

At the bottom of the pile was Ray Milner with the ball. The crowd was going crazy.

That's when the television camera focused on Jack Sutton, still on the ground, five yards from where the play had ended.

Reaching for his knee. Writhing in pain.

The television cameras showed the golf cart coming out of the tunnel about two minutes later, showed Alex Beech and Chuck Stoner, the other Bulldogs' linebackers, helping Jack onto the back of the cart. Every football fan watching knowing that a golf cart never meant anything good for the player about to get a ride on it out of the game.

"Same knee," Charlie said. "Same stinking knee."

The camera stayed on Jack Sutton and the cart until it

disappeared into the tunnel, out of sight, as the old man said, "He was the one always telling me you never know how many Sundays you're going to get."

Joe Warren paused and said, "Goes for all of us, doesn't it, Charlie boy?"

Anna called as soon as the half ended, Tom Pinkett having moved the Bulldogs into field goal range after Jack Sutton's injury, making the score 13–10.

"This stinks," she said.

"At least we're ahead," Charlie said.

"Sack getting hurt, I meant."

"I know what you meant," Charlie said. "But it doesn't mean we still can't win the second half without him."

"His season wasn't supposed to end like this."

"We just gotta make sure ours doesn't end, too."

Anna said, "I'm not calling again until we win, I'm afraid I might jinx us."

"Not gonna be anything *to* jinx."

"How's Gramps doing?"

"A lot better than me," Charlie said. "A couple of times I thought I should be the one attached to his heart monitor."

"Let's see if we can get through the third quarter with a lead," Anna said.

They didn't. The game went sideways on the Bulldogs' first series of the quarter, a blocked punt in the end zone putting Seattle ahead 17–13. Only a few plays later, the Seahawks got a pick six when Silas Burrell, coming out of the backfield, broke inside on a play he was supposed to take outside, nobody even close to the linebacker who took the gift pass and ran thirty yards down the sideline, straight into the end zone.

24–13, Seahawks.

Neither team scored the rest of the quarter. The Bulldogs opened up the fourth quarter with the ball, still trailing by eleven, their season on the line.

There was a knock on the door then, one of Mr. Warren's nurses poking her head in and asking if they wanted some company.

Then she was opening the door wide and Jack Sutton said he didn't need her help, he could wheel himself in. Jack Sutton wearing a Bulldogs sweatshirt over his hospital gown, his bad leg stretched out in front of him, ice taped to both sides of it, Jack explaining that the doctors had said all the pictures they wanted to take would be no good until they could get at least some of the swelling down.

"They think it's about half the alphabet," he said. "ACL, MCL." Gave a long look at Mr. Warren and said, "I'm done for good this time, Mr. Warren. I don't need the doctors to tell me the score."

The old man smiled at him. "But we're not, are we?"

"You sure?" Charlie said.

Jack Sutton moved his wheelchair to the left of Joe Warren then, Charlie staying where he was on the old man's right.

"It's like Mr. Warren keeps saying," Jack Sutton said to Charlie. "This is Hollywood. We all know how the movie's supposed to end."

Forty-Two

BOTH DEFENSES HAD REALLY SETTLED in now, neither offense able to generate more than one first down before punting. Bart Tubbs had replaced Jack and was playing the game of his life.

"Finally," Mr. Warren said.

"Finally what?" Jack said.

"I can finally remember why my son was so hot to draft the young man in the first place."

"Amen to that," Jack said.

And the old man said, "Is it time to resort to prayer? Because I can do that."

Tom Pinkett was limping a little himself now, having gone down hard a few minutes before on a safety blitz. But with two and a half minutes left, he somehow fought his way out of a defensive lineman's grasp, refusing to be sacked, and threw a prayer himself down the field toward Mo Bettencourt, who turned, leaped, and grabbed the ball out of the air. From there he simply fell forward, reaching out with the ball as it crossed the goal line. The side judge threw up both arms. Touchdown.

The extra point made it 24-20, Seattle.

"Onside kick?" Charlie said, thinking out loud.

"I don't think so, Charlie boy," the old man said. "I believe our coach is going to trust his defense. It's one of the things that has turned us around: Trust. They've started trusting each other again. I truly believe Coach Fiore will trust the defense to get him a stop now."

He was right. The kickoff went sailing right through the uprights. Coach Nick Fiore, they both knew, still had all his time-outs. If the Bulldogs could get him a stop, they could get the ball back with enough time to still win the game.

But if Colt Marley found a way to get his team a couple of first downs, the game was over, the season was over, no playoffs for the Bulldogs again, good-bye. So much had changed since September for the L.A. Bulldogs. But if they couldn't make something happen, *and right now*, they would finish out of the money again, as the old man liked to say.

And in that way, would be the Same Old Dogs.

On first down, the Seahawks ran the ball up the middle for a yard. Two-minute warning.

Nobody saying much of anything in Joe Warren's hospital room until Jack Sutton spoke.

"Blitz," he said when Colt Marley got under center, facing a second-and-nine.

"They'll run it again and make us burn a time-out, won't they?" Charlie said.

"The kid's going to run that pistol of his, make it look like a run, but he's going to throw for it," Jack said. "Get that first down and then make us burn *all* our time-outs. If he's gonna go for it, so should we. Throw the kitchen sink at him."

And that's exactly what the Bulldogs did, sending all three linebackers, do-or-die, Bart Tubbs leading the charge again as Marley recognized the blitz and scrambled as hard as he could to his right. But Bart was on him before he could even throw the ball away, seven-yard loss.

Third-and-sixteen. Minute and forty-eight seconds left. The Bulldogs called a time-out.

"Yes!" Jack Sutton yelled as he high-fived Joe Warren, maybe a little harder than he'd planned.

On third down, Colt Marley took the snap and fired a slant to his favorite receiver, Rashad Silver. Silver turned upfield and stretched as far as he could as the Bulldogs swarmed for the tackle.

He wound up a yard short. Fourth down.

Coach Nick Fiore called his last time-out with a minute and twenty left. The Seahawks punted.

Bulldogs' ball. Tom Pinkett's ball, no time-outs, seventy yards to go, just over a minute left at Bulldogs Stadium.

"Time to bring it home, old man," Jack Sutton said.

Charlie not sure in that moment whether he was talking about the owner of the Bulldogs or their quarterback.

Tom Pinkett wasted no time, looked like he had been waiting for this moment all game. The Seahawks were in a prevent defense, giving the Bulldog receivers chunks of yards in order to prevent a long pass for a touchdown. But after three first-down completions in a row, Tom had moved the ball all the way to the Seahawks' nine-yard line.

First-and-goal. The end zone, and the game, within reach. Twenty-four seconds left. The Seahawks' strong safety knocked down the pass intended for Mo Bettencourt over the middle on first down, Jack Sutton screaming that there should have been interference.

Second-and-goal. Eighteen seconds left.

Charlie jumped up out of his seat when Tom threw to Mo Bettencourt in the corner of the end zone on the next play, but Tom was just a little high and wide with the throw, the ball barely deflecting off of Mo's fingers.

Third-and-goal.

Thirteen seconds left.

Tom Pinkett worked out of the shotgun, took the ball, but nobody was open. He had to scramble to his left even on what was clearly a sore knee.

"Throw . . . it . . . away," Jack Sutton said.

Charlie thought he might try to run for it, even though the game would be over if he didn't make it. Like he had an idea about turning up the field and diving for the pylon.

Yet at the last second, he did what Jack wanted, throwing the ball over everybody.

Fourth down.

Five seconds left.

One play for everything.

"Who?" Jack Sutton said.

"Mo," Joe Warren said. "It's gotta be Mo. He's been our go-to guy all season."

"Agree," Jack Sutton said.

"No," Charlie said.

"*No?*" Jack Sutton said.

Charlie said, "Sometimes you go to your best guy, no doubt." He smiled and then quoted the last thing Tom Pinkett had said to him that day in the film room. "And sometimes you gotta throw them a curveball. Just to keep them on their toes."

"Boy sounds sure of himself," Jack Sutton said.

"Hasn't steered me wrong yet," Joe Warren said.

Without looking he put his hand out for Charlie, and Charlie squeezed it for all it was worth.

The old man's hand not feeling cold at all this time.

Tom was in the shotgun again, but the pocket seemed to collapse around him almost as soon as the ball was in his hands. The Seahawks came with their own all-out, do-or-die blitz.

But Tom Pinkett, even on a bad leg, cleared the pocket, looking at Mo the whole time on the left side, like it was Mo or nobody.

Then at the last second, as the game clock hit zero, just before he got absolutely buried, he turned, squared up, and threw across his body to the *right* corner of the end zone to Harrison Mays, wide open, for the touchdown pass that finally put Joe Warren and the Bulldogs into the NFL playoffs.

The only one in the room who could jump up was Charlie Gaines.

He came out of his chair as if he'd been shot out of it, and hugged Joe Warren, burying his head into his shoulder while Jack Sutton just kept yelling *"Oh yeah!"* over and over again.

Anna called then, Charlie's phone, doing a whole lot of yelling of her own, like she was trying to drown out Jack Sutton, Charlie feeling in that moment as if they were all together at Bulldogs Stadium after all.

"We did it we did it we did it!"

"We did it," Charlie said.

"We'll get there as soon as we can," Anna said. "For now, hug Gramps for me."

"Already did."

Jack Sutton said he'd be right back, he wanted to go get his phone, see if he could find a way to start calling the locker room, see which one of his teammates picked up.

Just Charlie and Joe Warren in the room now. The old man in his lucky chair, Charlie still next to him.

"Well, Charlie boy, if my heart can take that, I'm pretty sure it can take anything."

Charlie grinned. "Same," he said.

"We got the ending we wanted, didn't we?"

Charlie said, "We did. For now."

Then they were talking about the first-round of the playoffs, next Saturday or Sunday, Bulldogs Stadium, against the Packers, and how, if they could get by the Packers . . . well, anything was possible now, wasn't it?

"Like I kept telling you," the old man said. "You can't make it up, can you?"

And Charlie said, no sir, you sure couldn't make it up.

Not any of it.

Not even if you were the Fantasy King.

Forty- Three

THIS WAS THE AFTER-PARTY NOW, in Joe Warren's hospi-tal room, visiting hours having been extended for his family, Joe Warren having told the nurses on duty that both Anna and Char-lie were family.

It was just the three of them now, Anna's mom having gone home, saying she'd had all the fun she could handle for one day.

Matt Warren and Tom Pinkett had also left by now, but not before they had presented the game ball to Joe Warren.

The doctors had taken Jack Sutton downstairs for an MRI when the game was over even though there was still swelling around the knee, just so he could go home for the night. But Jack told the doctors that no amount of swelling was going to change what he knew had gone on inside his knee—that his career was really over this time.

Before he left he had stopped by the room one last time, on crutches now, to shake Joe Warren's hand and tell him that the Bulldogs weren't just making the playoffs, they were going all the way.

"Thanks for the opportunity, sir," he said.

"No," Joe Warren said. "Thank you."

So now it was just Joe Warren, Anna, and Charlie, the old man still sitting in his lucky chair, Anna on one side and Charlie on the other, all of them watching one postgame show after another, cheering every time Harrison Mays caught the winning pass.

"I was wrong about that last play, I thought he'd go back to Mo," Joe Warren said. "Never happier to be wrong in my life."

"I love it when Charlie is right, don't you, Gramps? Sometimes I love it sooooo much."

"Okay," Charlie said, "I'm not a dope. I'm missing some kind of private joke here, right?"

"What private joke could there be," Joe Warren said, "about an ending even more perfect than you know?"

"*More* perfect?" Charlie said. "Not possible."

He saw Anna smiling now, ear to ear. "Gramps, do you want to tell him, or shall I?"

"You mean, tell him that not only did Harrison win the game for us, he helped us win our league?"

"As in fantasy league, Charlie," Anna said. "For a little thing we like to think of as the Dream Team."

Charlie felt his mouth open, and then close. When it opened again he said, "No way."

"Way," Joe Warren said. "I told Anna at the start of the year it was about time to see what I was missing."

"I had to see if I could beat you just one stinking time," Anna said. "Head-to-head. And even though I would love to take credit, Gramps pretty much took charge."

Joe Warren said, "If Mo caught the last pass, I believe you would have won that league, Charlie boy. My heart nearly did stop when Tom gave that one last look to him. But then things ended exactly as they were supposed to."

Charlie thinking that to the end, the very end, he'd trusted his instincts this season, in big moments for both his teams. Because of the two big things Tom Pinkett had told him that day in the film room. Once, for the Culver City Cardinals, Charlie was sure the other team's quarterback would go back to his favorite receiver with a game on the line. And somehow today, Charlie had known that Tom was going to throw his curveball, go the other way, a curveball that became a perfect strike for the Los Angeles Bulldogs.

Joe Warren high-fived Anna then, who looked as cocky to Charlie as she ever had, which was saying something.

"Like I kept telling you in those e-mails all season, you will never beat me," she said. "Or beat *us*."

"You're the Dream Team," Charlie said, shaking his head.

"Well, *yeah*," Anna said. "Who's more of a dream team than Gramps and me?"

"Owner and girl general manager," Joe Warren said. "I mean, who knew how much fun fantasy football could be?"

"If I'd known it was you," Charlie said to Anna, "I would have figured out a way to win."

"Now you're the dreamer, Gaines," she said.

Why not? Charlie thought. It was all one big dream by now.

It was then that Joe Warren said he'd forgotten one last promise he'd made to Charlie, and asked the two of them to help him out of his chair, unhook him from his monitor, just for a moment.

When he was standing Anna said, "You sure you're good, Gramps?"

"You have no idea," he said.

Then he asked Charlie to give him the game ball. Told Charlie and Anna to give him some room.

The old man danced his touchdown dance then.

And was the youngest one in the room.

Acknowledgements

Zach Lupica and Andrew Gundling were my brains on fantasy football, and I am grateful to both of them.